The Boy Scout
And
Other Stories for Boys

Richard Harding Davis

The Boy Scout
And
Other Stories for Boys

Richard Harding Davis

THE BOY SCOUT AND OTHER STORIES FOR BOYS

THE BOY SCOUT

A Rule of the Boy Scouts is every day to do some one a good turn. Not because the copy-books tell you it deserves another, but in spite of that pleasing possibility. If you are a true Scout, until you have performed your act of kindness your day is dark. You are as unhappy as is the grown-up who has begun his day without shaving or reading the New York Sun. But as soon as you have proved yourself you may, with a clear conscience, look the world in the face and untie the knot in your kerchief.

Jimmie Reeder untied the accusing knot in his scarf at just ten minutes past eight on a hot August morning after he had given one dime to his sister Sadie. With that she could either witness the first-run films at the Palace, or dividing her fortune patronize two of the nickel shows on Lenox Avenue. The choice Jimmie left to her. He was setting out for the annual encampment of the Boy Scouts at Hunter's Island, and in the excitement of that adventure even the movies ceased to thrill. But Sadie also could be unselfish. With a heroism of a camp-fire maiden she made a gesture which might have been interpreted to mean she was returning the money.

"I can't, Jimmie!" she gasped. "I can't take it off you. You saved it, and you ought to get the fun of it."

"I haven't saved it yet," said Jimmie. "I'm going to cut it out of the railroad fare. I'm going to get off at City Island instead of at Pelham Manor and walk the difference. That's ten cents cheaper."

Sadie exclaimed with admiration:

"An' you carrying

' that heavy grip!"

"Aw, that's nothin'," said the man of the family.

"Good-by, mother. So long, Sadie."

To ward off further expressions of gratitude he hurriedly advised Sadie to take in "The Curse of Cain" rather than "The Mohawks' Last Stand," and fled down the front steps.

He wore his khaki uniform. On his shoulders was his knapsack, from his hands swung his suitcase and between his heavy stockings and his "shorts" his kneecaps, unkissed by the sun, as yet unscathed by blackberry vines, showed as white and fragile as the wrists of a girl. As he moved toward the "L" station at the corner, Sadie and his mother waved to him; in the street, boys too small to be Scouts hailed him enviously; even the policeman glancing over the newspapers on the news-stand nodded approval.

"You a Scout, Jimmie?" he asked.

"No," retorted Jimmie, for was not he also in uniform? "I'm Santa Claus out filling Christmas stockings."

The patrolman also possessed a ready wit.

"Then get yourself a pair," he advised. "If a dog was to see your legs—"

Jimmie escaped the insult by fleeing up the steps of the Elevated.

An hour later, with his valise in one hand and staff in the other, he was tramping up the Boston Post Road and breathing heavily. The day was cruelly hot. Before his eyes, over an interminable stretch of asphalt, the heat waves danced and flickered. Already the knapsack on his shoulders pressed upon him like an Old Man of the Sea; the linen in the valise had turned to pig iron, his pipe-stem legs were wabbling, his eyes smarted with salt sweat, and the fingers supporting the valise belonged to some other boy, and were giving that boy much pain. But as the motor-cars flashed past with raucous warnings, or, that those who rode might better see the boy with bare knees, passed at "half speed," Jimmie stiffened his shoulders and stepped jauntily forward. Even when the joy-riders mocked with "Oh, you Scout!" he smiled at them. He was willing to admit to those who rode that the laugh was on the one who walked. And he regretted–oh, so bitterly–having left the train. He was indignant that for his "one good turn a day" he had not selected one less strenuous. That, for instance, he had not assisted a frightened old lady through the traffic. To refuse the dime she might have offered, as all true Scouts refuse all tips, would have been easier than to earn it by walking five miles, with the sun at ninety-nine degrees, and carrying excess baggage. Twenty times James shifted the valise to the other hand, twenty times he let it drop and sat upon it.

And then, as again he took up his burden, the Good Samaritan drew near. He drew near in a low gray racing-car at the rate of forty miles an hour, and within a hundred feet of Jimmie suddenly stopped and backed toward him. The Good Samaritan was a young man with white hair. He wore a suit of blue, a golf cap; the hands that held the wheel were disguised in large yellow gloves. He brought the car to a halt and surveyed the dripping figure in the road with tired and uncurious eyes.

"You a Boy Scout?" he asked.

Jimmie dropped the valise, forced his cramped fingers into straight lines, and saluted.

With alacrity for the twenty-first time Jimmie dropped the valise, forced his cramped fingers into straight lines, and saluted.

The young man in the car nodded toward the seat beside him.

"Get in," he commanded.

When James sat panting happily at his elbow the old young man, to Jimmie's disappointment, did not continue to shatter the speed limit. Instead, he seemed inclined for conversation, and the car, growling indignantly, crawled.

"I never saw a Boy Scout before," announced the old young man. "Tell me about it. First, tell me what you do when you're not scouting."

Jimmie explained volubly. When not in uniform he was an office-boy and from pedlers and beggars guarded the gates of Carroll and Hastings, stock-brokers. He spoke the names of his employers with awe. It was a firm distinguished, conservative, and long-established. The white-haired young man seemed to nod in assent.

"Do you know them?" demanded Jimmie suspiciously. "Are you a customer of ours?"

"I know them," said the young man. "They are customers of mine."

Jimmie wondered in what way Carroll and Hastings were customers of the white-haired young man. Judging him by his outer garments, Jimmie guessed he was a Fifth Avenue tailor; he might be even a haberdasher. Jimmie continued. He lived, he explained, with his mother at One Hundred and Forty-sixth Street; Sadie, his sister, attended the public school; he helped support them both, and he now was about to enjoy a well-earned vacation camping out on Hunter's Island, where he would cook his own meals and, if the mosquitoes permitted, sleep in a tent.

"And you like that?" demanded the young man. "You call that fun?"

"Sure!" protested Jimmie. "Don't you go camping out?"

"I go camping out," said the Good Samaritan, "whenever I leave New York."

Jimmie had not for three years lived in Wall Street not to understand that the young man spoke in metaphor.

"You don't look," objected the young man critically, "as though you were built for the strenuous life."

Jimmie glanced guiltily at his white knees.

"You ought ter see me two weeks from now," he protested. "I get all sunburnt and hard–hard as anything!"

The young man was incredulous.

"You were near getting sunstroke when I picked you up," he laughed. "If you're going to Hunter's Island why didn't you take the Third Avenue to Pelham Manor?"

"That's right!" assented Jimmie eagerly. "But I wanted to save the ten cents so's to send Sadie to the movies. So I walked."

The young man looked his embarrassment.

"I beg your pardon," he murmured.

But Jimmie did not hear him. From the back of the car he was dragging excitedly at the hated suitcase.

"Stop!" he commanded. "I got ter get out. I got ter walk."

The young man showed his surprise.

"Walk!" he exclaimed. "What is it–a bet?"

Jimmie dropped the valise and followed it into the roadway. It took some time to explain to the young man. First, he had to be told about the scout law and the one good turn a day, and that it must involve some personal sacrifice. And, as Jimmie pointed out, changing from a slow suburban train to a racing-car could not be listed as a sacrifice. He had not earned the money, Jimmie argued; he had only avoided paying it to the railroad. If he did not walk he would be obtaining the gratitude of Sadie by a falsehood. Therefore, he must walk.

"Not at all," protested the young man. "You've got it wrong. What good will it do your sister to have you sunstruck? I think you are sunstruck. You're crazy with the heat. You get in here, and we'll talk it over as we go along."

Hastily Jimmie backed away. "I'd rather walk," he said.

The young man shifted his legs irritably.

"Then how'll this suit you?" he called. "We'll declare that first 'one good turn' a failure and start afresh. Do me a good turn."

Jimmie halted in his tracks and looked back suspiciously.

"I'm going to Hunter's Island Inn," called the young man, "and I've lost my way. You get in here and guide me. That'll be doing me a good turn."

On either side of the road, blotting out the landscape, giant hands picked out in electric-light bulbs pointed the way to Hunter's Island Inn. Jimmie grinned and nodded toward them.

"Much obliged," he called, "I got ter walk." Turning his back upon temptation, he wabbled forward into the flickering heat waves.

The young man did not attempt to pursue. At the side of the road, under the shade of a giant elm, he had brought the car to a halt and with his arms crossed upon the wheel sat motionless, following with frowning eyes the retreating figure of Jimmie. But the narrow-chested and knock-kneed boy staggering over the sun-baked asphalt no longer concerned him. It was not Jimmie, but the code preached by Jimmie, and not only preached but before his eyes put into practice, that interested him. The young man with white hair had been running away from temptation. At forty miles an hour he had been running away from the temptation to do a fellow mortal "a good turn." That morning, to the appeal of a drowning Cæsar to "Help me, Cassius, or I sink," he had answered, "Sink!" That answer he had no wish to reconsider. That he might not reconsider he had sought to escape. It was his experience that a sixty-horse-power racing-machine is a jealous mistress. For retrospective, sentimental, or philanthropic thoughts she grants no leave of absence. But he had not escaped. Jimmie had halted him, tripped him by the heels and set him again to thinking. Within the half-hour that followed those who rolled past saw at the side of the road a car with her engine running, and leaning upon the wheel, as unconscious of his surroundings as though he sat at his own fireplace, a young man who frowned and stared at nothing. The half-hour passed and the young man swung his car back toward the city. But at the first roadhouse that showed a blue-and-white telephone sign he left it, and into the iron box at the end of the bar dropped a nickel. He wished to communicate with Mr. Carroll, of Carroll and Hastings; and when he learned Mr. Carroll had just issued orders that he must not be disturbed, the young man gave his name.

The effect upon the barkeeper was instantaneous. With the aggrieved air of one who feels he is the victim of a jest he laughed scornfully. "What are you putting over?" he demanded.

The young man smiled reassuringly. He had begun to speak and, though apparently engaged with the beer-glass he was polishing, the barkeeper listened.

Down in Wall Street the senior member of Carroll and Hastings also listened. He was alone in the most private of all his private offices, and when interrupted had been engaged in what, of all undertakings, is the most momentous. On the desk before him lay letters to his lawyer, to the coroner, to his wife; and hidden by a mass of papers, but within reach of his hand, an automatic pistol. The promise it offered of swift release had made the writing of the letters simple, had given him a feeling of complete detachment, had released him, at least in thought, from all responsibilities. And when at his elbow the telephone coughed discreetly, it was as though some one had called him from a world from which already he had made his exit.

Mechanically, through mere habit, he lifted the receiver.

The voice over the telephone came in brisk staccato sentences.

"That letter I sent this morning? Forget it. Tear it up. I've been thinking and I'm going to take a chance. I've decided to back you boys, and I know you'll make good. I'm speaking from a roadhouse in the Bronx; going straight from here to the bank. So you can begin to draw against us within an hour. And–

hello!–will three millions see you through?"

From Wall Street there came no answer, but from the hands of the barkeeper a glass crashed to the floor.

The young man regarded the barkeeper with puzzled eyes.

"He doesn't answer," he exclaimed. "He must have hung up."

"He must have fainted!" said the barkeeper.

The white-haired one pushed a bill across the counter. "To pay for breakage," he said, and disappeared down Pelham Parkway.

Throughout the day, with the bill, for evidence, pasted against the mirror, the barkeeper told and retold the wondrous tale.

"He stood just where you're standing now," he related, "blowing in million-dollar bills like you'd blow suds off a beer. If I'd knowed it was him, I'd have hit him once, and hid him in the cellar for the reward. Who'd I think he was? I thought he was a wire-tapper, working a con game!"

Mr. Carroll had not "hung up," but when in the Bronx the beer-glass crashed, in Wall Street the receiver had slipped from the hand of the man who held it, and the man himself had fallen forward. His desk hit him in the face and woke him–woke him to the wonderful fact that he still lived; that at forty he had been born again; that before him stretched many more years in which, as the young man with the white hair had pointed out, he still could make good.

The afternoon was far advanced when the staff of Carroll and Hastings were allowed to depart, and, even late as was the hour, two of them were asked to remain. Into the most private of the private offices Carroll invited Gaskell, the head clerk; in the main office Hastings had asked young Thorne, the bond clerk, to be seated.

Until the senior partner has finished with Gaskell young Thorne must remain seated.

"Gaskell," said Mr. Carroll, "if we had listened to you, if we'd run this place as it was when father was alive, this never would have happened. It hasn't happened, but we've had our lesson. And after this we're going slow and going straight. And we don't need you to tell us how to do that. We want you to go away–on a month's vacation. When I thought we were going under I planned to send the children on a sea-voyage with the governess–so they wouldn't see the newspapers. But now that I can look them in the eye again, I need them, I can't let them go. So, if you'd like to take your wife on an ocean trip to Nova Scotia and Quebec, here are the cabins I reserved for the kids. They call it the Royal Suite–whatever that is–and the trip lasts a month. The boat sails to-morrow morning. Don't sleep too late or you may miss her."

The head clerk was secreting the tickets in the inside pocket of his waistcoat. His fingers trembled, and when he laughed his voice trembled.

"Miss the boat!" the head clerk exclaimed. "If she gets away from Millie and me she's got to start now. We'll go on board to-night!"

A half-hour later Millie was on her knees packing a trunk, and her husband was telephoning to the drug-store for a sponge bag and a cure for sea-sickness.

Owing to the joy in her heart and to the fact that she was on her knees, Millie was alternately weeping into the trunk-tray and offering up incoherent prayers of thanksgiving. Suddenly she sank back upon the floor.

"John!" she cried, "doesn't it seem sinful to sail away in a 'royal suite' and leave this beautiful flat empty?"

Over the telephone John was having trouble with the drug clerk.

"No!" he explained, "I'm not sea-sick now. The medicine I want is to be taken later. I know I'm speaking from the Pavonia; but the Pavonia isn't a ship; it's an apartment-house."

He turned to Millie. "We can't be in two places at the same time," he suggested.

"But, think," insisted Millie, "of all the poor people stifling to-night in this heat, trying to sleep on the roofs and fire-escapes; and our flat so cool and big and pretty–and no one in it."

John nodded his head proudly.

"I know it's big," he said, "but it isn't big enough to hold all the people who are sleeping to-night on the roofs and in the parks."

"I was thinking of your brother–and Grace," said Millie. "They've been married only two weeks now, and they're in a stuffy hall bedroom and eating with all the other boarders. Think what our flat would mean to them; to be by themselves, with eight rooms and their own kitchen and bath, and our new refrigerator and the gramophone! It would be Heaven! It would be a real honeymoon!"

Abandoning the drug clerk, John lifted Millie in his arms and kissed her, for next to his wife nearest his heart was the younger brother.

The younger brother and Grace were sitting on the stoop of the boarding-house. On the upper steps, in their shirt-sleeves, were the other boarders; so the bride and bridegroom spoke in whispers. The air of the cross street was stale and stagnant; from it rose exhalations of rotting fruit, the gases of an open subway, the smoke of passing taxicabs. But between the street and the hall bedroom, with its odors of a gas-stove and a kitchen, the choice was difficult.

"We've got to cool off somehow," the young husband was saying, "or you won't sleep. Shall we treat ourselves to ice-cream sodas or a trip on the Weehawken ferry-boat?"

"The ferry-boat!" begged the girl, "where we can get away from all these people."

A taxicab with a trunk in front whirled into the street, kicked itself to a stop, and the head clerk and Millie spilled out upon the pavement. They talked so fast, and the younger brother and Grace talked so fast, that the boarders, although they listened intently, could make nothing of it.

They distinguished only the concluding sentences:

"Why don't you drive down to the wharf with us," they heard the elder brother ask, "and see our royal suite?"

But the younger brother laughed him to scorn.

"What's your royal suite," he mocked, "to our royal palace?"

An hour later, had the boarders listened outside the flat of the head clerk, they would have heard issuing from his bathroom the cooling murmur of running water and from his gramophone the jubilant notes of "Alexander's Ragtime Band."

When in his private office Carroll was making a present of the royal suite to the head clerk, in the main office Hastings, the junior partner, was addressing "Champ" Thorne, the bond clerk. He addressed him familiarly and affectionately as "Champ." This was due partly to the fact that twenty-six years before Thorne had been christened Champneys and to the coincidence that he had captained the football eleven of one of the Big Three to the championship.

"Champ," said Mr. Hastings, "last month, when you asked me to raise your salary, the reason I didn't do it was not because you didn't deserve it, but because I believed if we gave you a raise you'd immediately get married."

The shoulders of the ex-football captain rose aggressively; he snorted with indignation.

"And why should I not get married?" he demanded. "You're a fine one to talk! You're the most offensively happy married man I ever met."

"Perhaps I know I am happy better than you do," reproved the junior partner; "but I know also that it takes money to support a wife."

"You raise me to a hundred a week," urged Champ, "and I'll make it support a wife whether it supports me or not."

"A month ago," continued Hastings, "we could have promised you a hundred, but we didn't know how long we could pay it. We didn't want you to rush off and marry some fine girl—"

"Some fine girl!" muttered Mr. Thorne. "The Finest Girl!"

"The finer the girl," Hastings pointed out, "the harder it would have been for you if we had failed and you had lost your job."

The eyes of the young man opened with sympathy and concern.

"Is it as bad as that?" he murmured.

Hastings sighed happily.

"It was," he said, "but this morning the Young Man of Wall Street did us a good turn–saved us–saved our creditors, saved our homes, saved our honor. We're going to start fresh and pay our debts, and we agreed the first debt we paid would be the small one we owe you. You've brought us more than we've given, and if you'll stay with us we're going to 'see' your fifty and raise it a hundred. What do you say?"

Young Mr. Thorne leaped to his feet. What he said was: "Where'n hell's my hat?"

But by the time he had found the hat and the door he mended his manners.

"I say, 'thank you a thousand times,'" he shouted over his shoulder. "Excuse me, but I've got to go. I've got to break the news to—"

He did not explain to whom he was going to break the news; but Hastings must have guessed, for again he sighed happily and then, a little hysterically, laughed aloud. Several months had passed since he had laughed aloud.

In his anxiety to break the news Champ Thorne almost broke his neck. In his excitement he could not remember whether the red flash meant the elevator was going down or coming up, and sooner than wait to find out he started to race down eighteen flights of stairs when fortunately the elevator-door swung open.

"You get five dollars," he announced to the elevator man, "if you drop to the street without a stop. Beat the speed limit! Act like the building is on fire and you're trying to save me before the roof falls."

Senator Barnes and his entire family, which was his daughter Barbara, were at the Ritz-Carlton. They were in town in August because there was a meeting of the directors of the Brazil and Cuyaba Rubber Company, of which company Senator Barnes was president. It was a secret meeting. Those directors who were keeping cool at the edge of the ocean had been summoned by telegraph; those who were steaming across the ocean, by wireless.

Up from the equator had drifted the threat of a scandal, sickening, grim, terrible. As yet it burned beneath the surface, giving out only an odor, but an odor as rank as burning rubber itself. At any moment it might break into flame. For the directors, was it the better wisdom to let the scandal smoulder, and take a chance, or to be the first to give the alarm, the first to lead the way to the horror and stamp it out?

It was to decide this that, in the heat of August, the directors and the president had foregathered.

Champ Thorne knew nothing of this; he knew only that by a miracle Barbara Barnes was in town; that at last he was in a position to ask her to marry him; that she would certainly say she would. That was all he cared to know.

A year before he had issued his declaration of independence. Before he could marry, he told her, he must be able to support a wife on what he earned, without her having to accept money from her father, and until he received "a minimum wage" of five thousand dollars they must wait.

"What is the matter with my father's money?" Barbara had demanded.

Thorne had evaded the direct question.

"There is too much of it," he said.

"Do you object to the way he makes it?" insisted Barbara. "Because rubber is most useful. You put it in golf balls and auto tires and galoches. There is nothing so perfectly respectable as galoches. And what is there 'tainted' about a raincoat?"

Thorne shook his head unhappily.

"It's not the finished product to which I refer," he stammered; "it's the way they get the raw material."

"They get it out of trees," said Barbara. Then she exclaimed with enlightenment—"Oh!" she cried, "you are thinking of the Congo. There it is terrible! That is slavery. But there are no slaves on the Amazon. The natives are free and the work is easy. They just tap the trees the way the farmers gather sugar in Vermont. Father has told me about it often."

Thorne had made no comment. He could abuse a friend, if the friend were among those present, but denouncing any one he disliked as heartily as he disliked Senator Barnes was a public service he preferred to leave to others. And he knew besides that, if the father she loved and the man she loved distrusted each other, Barbara would not rest until she learned the reason why.

One day, in a newspaper, Barbara read of the Puju Mayo atrocities, of the Indian slaves in the jungles and back waters of the Amazon, who are offered up as sacrifices to "red rubber." She carried the paper to her father. What it said, her father told her, was untrue, and if it were true it was the first he had heard of it.

Senator Barnes loved the good things of life, but the thing he loved most was his daughter; the thing he valued the highest was her good opinion. So when for the first time she looked at him in doubt, he assured her he at once would order an investigation.

"But, of course," he added, "it will be many months before our agents can report. On the Amazon news travels very slowly."

In the eyes of his daughter the doubt still lingered.

"I am afraid," she said, "that that is true."

That was six months before the directors of the Brazil and Cuyaba Rubber Company were summoned to meet their president at his rooms in the Ritz-Carlton. They were due to arrive in half an hour, and while Senator Barnes awaited their coming Barbara came to him. In her eyes was a light that helped to tell the great news. It gave him a sharp, jealous pang. He wanted at once to play a part in her happiness, to make her grateful to him, not alone to this stranger who was taking her away. So fearful was he that she would shut him out of her life that had she asked for half his kingdom he would have parted with it.

"And besides giving my consent," said the rubber king, "for which no one seems to have asked, what can I give my little girl to make her remember her old father? Some diamonds to put on her head, or pearls to hang around her neck, or does she want a vacant lot on Fifth Avenue?"

The lovely hands of Barbara rested upon his shoulders; her lovely face was raised to his; her lovely eyes were appealing, and a little frightened.

"What would one of those things cost?" asked Barbara.

The question was eminently practical. It came within the scope of the senator's understanding. After all, he was not to be cast into outer darkness. His smile was complacent. He answered airily:

"Anything you like," he said; "a million dollars?"

The fingers closed upon his shoulders. The eyes, still frightened, still searched his in appeal.

"Then for my wedding-present," said the girl, "I want you to take that million dollars and send an expedition to the Amazon. And I will choose the men. Men unafraid; men not afraid of fever or sudden death; not afraid to tell the truth–even to you. And all the world will know. And they–I mean you–will set those people free!"

Senator Barnes received the directors with an embarrassment which he concealed under a manner of just indignation.

"My mind is made up," he told them. "Existing conditions cannot continue. And to that end, at my own expense, I am sending an expedition across South America. It will investigate, punish, and establish reforms. I suggest, on account of this damned heat, we do now adjourn."

That night, over on Long Island, Carroll told his wife all, or nearly all. He did not tell her about the automatic pistol. And together on tiptoe they crept to the nursery and looked down at their sleeping children. When she rose from her knees the mother said, "But how can I thank him?"

By "him" she meant the Young Man of Wall Street.

"You never can thank him," said Carroll; "that's the worst of it."

But after a long silence the mother said: "I will send him a photograph of the children. Do you think he will understand?"

Down at Seabright, Hastings and his wife walked in the sunken garden. The moon was so bright that the roses still held their color.

"I would like to thank him," said the young wife. She meant the Young Man of Wall Street. "But for him we would have lost this."

Her eyes caressed the garden, the fruit-trees, the house with wide, hospitable verandas. "To-morrow I will send him some of these roses," said the young wife. "Will he understand that they mean our home?"

At a scandalously late hour, in a scandalous spirit of independence, Champ Thorne and Barbara were driving around Central Park in a taxicab.

"How strangely the Lord moves, his wonders to perform," misquoted Barbara. "Had not the Young Man of Wall Street saved Mr. Hastings, Mr. Hastings could not have raised your salary; you would not have asked me to marry you, and had you not asked me to marry you, father would not have given me a wedding-present, and—"

"And," said Champ, taking up the tale, "thousands of slaves would still be buried in the jungles, hidden away from their wives and children, and the light of the sun and their fellow men. They still would be dying of fever, starvation, tortures."

He took her hand in both of his and held her finger-tips against his lips.

"And they will never know," he whispered, "when their freedom comes, that they owe it all to you."

On Hunter's Island Jimmie Reeder and his bunkie, Sam Sturges, each on his canvas cot, tossed and twisted. The heat, the moonlight, and the mosquitoes would not let them even think of sleep.

"That was bully," said Jimmie, "what you did to-day about saving that dog. If it hadn't been for you he'd ha' drownded."

"He would not!" said Sammy with punctilious regard for the truth; "it wasn't deep enough."

"Well, the scout-master ought to know," argued Jimmie; "he said it was the best 'one good turn' of the day!"

Modestly Sam shifted the limelight so that it fell upon his bunkie.

"I'll bet," he declared loyally, "your 'one good turn' was a better one!"

Jimmie yawned, and then laughed scornfully.

"Me," he scoffed, "I didn't do nothing. I sent my sister to the movies."

THE BOY WHO CRIED WOLF

Before he finally arrested him, "Jimmie" Sniffen had seen the man with the golf-cap, and the blue eyes that laughed at you, three times. Twice, unexpectedly, he had come upon him in a wood road and once on Round Hill where the stranger was pretending to watch the sunset. Jimmie knew people do not climb hills merely to look at sunsets, so he was not deceived. He guessed the man was a German spy seeking gun sites, and secretly vowed to "stalk" him. From that moment, had the stranger known it, he was as good as dead. For a boy scout with badges on his sleeve for "stalking" and "path-finding," not to boast of others for "gardening" and "cooking," can outwit any spy. Even had General Baden-Powell remained in Mafeking and not invented the boy scout, Jimmie Sniffen would have been one. Because by birth he was a boy, and by inheritance a scout. In Westchester County the Sniffens are one of the county families. If it isn't a Sarles, it's a Sniffen; and with Brundages, Platts, and Jays, the Sniffens date back to when the acres of the first Charles Ferris ran from the Boston post road to the coach road to Albany, and when the first Gouverneur Morris stood on one of his hills and saw the Indian canoes in the Hudson and in the Sound and rejoiced that all the land between belonged to him.

If you do not believe in heredity, the fact that Jimmie's great-great-grandfather was a scout for General Washington and hunted deer, and even bear, over exactly the same hills where Jimmie hunted weasels will count for nothing. It will not explain why to Jimmie, from Tarrytown to Port Chester, the hills, the roads, the woods, and the cowpaths, caves, streams, and springs hidden in the woods were as familiar as his own kitchen garden.

Nor explain why, when you could not see a Pease and Elliman "For Sale" sign nailed to a tree, Jimmie could see in the highest branches a last year's bird's nest.

Or why, when he was out alone playing Indians and had sunk his scout's axe into a fallen log and then scalped the log, he felt that once before in those same woods he had trailed that same Indian, and with his own tomahawk split open his skull. Sometimes when he knelt to drink at a secret spring in the forest, the autumn leaves would crackle and he would raise his eyes fearing to see a panther facing him.

"But there ain't no panthers in Westchester," Jimmie would reassure himself. And in the distance the roar of an automobile climbing a hill with the muffler open would seem to suggest he was right. But still Jimmie remembered once before he had knelt at that same spring, and that when he raised his eyes he had faced a crouching panther. "Mebbe dad told me it happened to grandpop," Jimmie would explain, "or I dreamed it, or, mebbe, I read it in a story book."

The "German spy" mania attacked Round Hill after the visit to the boy scouts of Clavering Gould, the war correspondent. He was spending the week-end with "Squire" Harry Van Vorst, and as young Van Vorst, besides being a justice of the peace and a Master of Beagles and President of the Country Club, was also a local "councilman" for the Round Hill Scouts, he brought his guest to a camp-fire meeting to talk to them. In deference to his audience, Gould told them of the boy scouts he had seen in Belgium and of the part they were playing in the great war. It was his peroration that made trouble.

"And any day," he assured his audience, "this country may be at war with Germany; and every one of you boys will be expected to do his bit. You can begin now. When the Germans land it will be near New Haven, or New Bedford. They will first capture the munition works at Springfield, Hartford, and Watervliet so as to make sure of their ammunition, and then they will start for New York City. They will follow the New Haven and New York Central railroads, and march straight through this village. I haven't the least doubt," exclaimed the enthusiastic war prophet, "that at this moment German spies are as thick in Westchester as blackberries. They are here to select camp sites and gun positions, to find out which of these hills enfilade the others and to learn to what extent their armies can live on the country. They are counting the cows, the horses, the barns where fodder is stored; and they are marking down on their maps the wells and streams."

As though at that moment a German spy might be crouching behind the door, Mr. Gould spoke in a whisper. "Keep your eyes open!" he commanded. "Watch every stranger. If he acts suspiciously, get word quick to your sheriff, or to Judge Van Vorst here. Remember the scouts' motto, 'Be prepared!'"

That night as the scouts walked home, behind each wall and hayrick they saw spiked helmets.

Young Van Vorst was extremely annoyed.

"Next time you talk to my scouts," he declared, "you'll talk on 'Votes for Women.' After what you said to-night every real-estate agent who dares open a map will be arrested. We're not trying to drive people away from Westchester, we're trying to sell them building sites."

"You are not!" retorted his friend, "you own half the county now, and you're trying to buy the other half."

"I'm a justice of the peace," explained Van Vorst. "I don't know why I am, except that they wished it on me. All I get out of it is trouble. The Italians make charges against my best friends for over-speeding, and I have to fine them, and my best friends bring charges against the Italians for poaching, and when I fine the Italians they send me Black Hand letters. And now every day I'll be asked to issue a warrant for a German spy who is selecting gun sites. And he will turn out to be a millionaire who is tired of living at the Ritz-Carlton and wants to 'own his own home' and his own golf-links. And he'll be so hot at being arrested that he'll take his millions to Long Island and try to break into the Piping Rock Club. And it will be your fault!"

The young justice of the peace was right. At least so far as Jimmie Sniffen was concerned, the words of the war prophet had filled one mind with unrest. In the past Jimmie's idea of a holiday had been to spend it scouting in the woods. In this pleasure he was selfish. He did not want companions who talked, and trampled upon the dead leaves so that they frightened the wild animals and gave the Indians warning. Jimmie liked to pretend. He liked to fill the woods with wary and hostile adversaries. It was a game of his own inventing. If he crept to the top of a hill and, on peering over it, surprised a fat woodchuck, he pretended the woodchuck was a bear, weighing two hundred pounds; if, himself unobserved, he could lie and watch, off its guard, a rabbit, squirrel, or, most difficult of all, a crow, it became a deer and that night at supper Jimmie made believe he was eating venison. Sometimes he was a scout of the Continental Army and carried despatches to General Washington. The rules of that game were that if any man ploughing in the fields, or cutting trees in the woods, or even approaching along the same road, saw Jimmie before Jimmie saw him, Jimmie was taken prisoner, and before sunrise was shot as a spy. He was seldom shot. Or else why on his sleeve was the badge for "stalking"? But always to have to make believe became monotonous. Even "dry shopping" along the Rue de la Paix, when you pretend you can have anything you see in any window, leaves one just as rich, but unsatisfied. So the advice of the war correspondent to seek out German spies came to Jimmie like a day at the circus, like a week at the Danbury Fair. It not only was a call to arms, to protect his flag and home, but a chance to play in earnest the game in which he most delighted. No longer need he pretend. No longer need he waste his energies in watching, unobserved, a greedy rabbit rob a carrot field. The game now was his fellow-man and his enemy; not only his enemy, but the enemy of his country.

In his first effort Jimmie was not entirely successful. The man looked the part perfectly; he wore an auburn beard, disguising spectacles, and he carried a suspicious knapsack. But he turned out to be a professor from the Museum of Natural History, who wanted to dig for Indian arrow-heads. And when Jimmie threatened to arrest him, the indignant gentleman arrested Jimmie. Jimmie escaped only by leading the professor to a secret cave of his own, though on some one else's property, where one not only could dig for arrow-heads, but find them. The professor was delighted, but for Jimmie it was a great disappointment. The week following Jimmie was again disappointed.

On the bank of the Kensico Reservoir, he came upon a man who was acting in a mysterious and suspicious manner. He was making notes in a book, and his runabout which he had concealed in a wood road was stuffed with blue-prints. It did not take Jimmie long to guess his purpose. He was planning to blow up the Kensico dam, and cut off the water supply of New York City. Seven millions of people without water! Without firing a shot, New York must surrender! At the thought Jimmie shuddered, and at the risk of his life, by clinging to the tail of a motor truck, he followed the runabout into White Plains. But there it developed the mysterious stranger, so far from wishing to destroy the Kensico dam, was the State Engineer who had built it, and, also, a large part of the Panama Canal. Nor in his third effort was Jimmie more successful. From the heights of Pound Ridge he discovered on a hilltop below him a man working along upon a basin of concrete. The man was a German-American, and already on Jimmie's list of "suspects." That for the use of the German artillery he was preparing a concrete bed for a siege gun was only too evident. But closer investigation proved that the concrete was only two inches thick. And the hyphenated one explained that the basin was built over a spring, in the waters of which he planned to erect a fountain and raise goldfish. It was a bitter blow. Jimmie became discouraged. Meeting Judge Van Vorst one day in the road he told him his troubles. The young judge proved unsympathetic. "My advice to you, Jimmie," he said, "is to go slow. Accusing everybody of espionage is a very serious matter. If you call a man a spy, it's sometimes hard for him to disprove it; and the name sticks. So, go slow–very slow. Before you arrest any more people, come to me first for a warrant."

So, the next time Jimmie proceeded with caution.

Besides being a farmer in a small way, Jimmie's father was a handy man with tools. He had no union card, but, in laying shingles along a blue chalk line, few were as expert. It was August, there was no school, and Jimmie was carrying a dinner-pail to where his father was at work on a new barn. He made a cross-cut through the woods, and came upon the young man in the golf-cap. The stranger nodded, and his eyes, which seemed to be always laughing, smiled pleasantly. But he was deeply tanned, and, from the waist up, held himself like a soldier, so, at once, Jimmie mistrusted him. Early the next morning Jimmie met him again. It had not been raining, but the clothes of the young man were damp. Jimmie guessed that while the dew was still on the leaves the young man had been forcing his way through underbrush. The stranger must have remembered Jimmie, for he laughed and exclaimed:

"Ah, my friend with the dinner-pail! It's luck you haven't got it now, or I'd hold you up. I'm starving!"

Jimmie smiled in sympathy. "It's early to be hungry," said Jimmie; "when did you have your breakfast?"

"I didn't," laughed the young man. "I went out to walk up an appetite, and I lost myself. But I haven't lost my appetite. Which is the shortest way back to Bedford?"

"The first road to your right," said Jimmie.

"Is it far?" asked the stranger anxiously. That he was very hungry was evident.

"It's a half-hour's walk," said Jimmie.

"If I live that long," corrected the young man; and stepped out briskly.

Jimmie knew that within a hundred yards a turn in the road would shut him from sight. So, he gave the stranger time to walk that distance, and then, diving into the wood that lined the road, "stalked" him. From behind a tree he saw the stranger turn and look back, and seeing no one in the road behind him, also leave it and plunge into the woods.

He had not turned toward Bedford; he had turned to the left. Like a runner stealing bases, Jimmie slipped from tree to tree. Ahead of him he heard the stranger trampling upon dead twigs, moving rapidly as one who knew his way. At times through the branches Jimmie could see the broad shoulders of the stranger, and again could follow his progress only by the noise of the crackling twigs. When the noises ceased, Jimmie guessed the stranger had reached the wood road, grass-grown and moss-covered, that led to Middle Patent. So, he ran at right angles until he also reached it, and as now he was close to where it entered the main road, he approached warily. But he was too late. There was a sound like the whir of a rising partridge, and ahead of him from where it had been hidden, a gray touring-car leaped into the highway. The stranger was at the wheel. Throwing behind it a cloud of dust, the car raced toward Greenwich. Jimmie had time to note only that it bore a Connecticut State license; that in the wheel-ruts the tires printed little V's, like arrow-heads.

For a week Jimmie saw nothing of the spy, but for many hot and dusty miles he stalked arrow-heads. They lured him north, they lured him south, they were stamped in soft asphalt, in mud, dust, and fresh-spread tarvia. Wherever Jimmie walked, arrow-heads ran before. In his sleep as in his copy-book, he saw endless chains of V's. But not once could he catch up with the wheels that printed them. A week later, just at sunset as he passed below Round Hill, he saw the stranger on top of it. On the skyline, in silhouette against the sinking sun, he was as conspicuous as a flagstaff. But to approach him was impossible. For acres Round Hill offered no other cover than stubble. It was as bald as a skull. Until the stranger chose to descend, Jimmie must wait. And the stranger was in no haste. The sun sank and from the west Jimmie saw him turn his face east toward the Sound. A storm was gathering, drops of rain began to splash and as the sky grew black the figure on the hilltop faded into the darkness. And then, at the very spot where Jimmie had last seen it, there suddenly flared two tiny flashes of fire. Jimmie leaped from cover. It was no longer to be endured. The spy was signalling. The time for caution had passed, now was the time to act. Jimmie raced to the top of the hill, and found it empty. He plunged down it, vaulted a stone wall, forced his way through a tangle of saplings, and held his breath to listen. Just beyond him, over a jumble of rocks, a hidden stream was tripping and tumbling. Joyfully it laughed and gurgled. Jimmie turned hot. It sounded as though from the darkness the spy mocked him. Jimmie shook his fist at the enshrouding darkness. Above the tumult of the coming storm and the tossing tree-tops, he raised his voice.

"You wait!" he shouted. "I'll get you yet! Next time, I'll bring a gun."

Next time was the next morning. There had been a hawk hovering over the chicken yard, and Jimmie used that fact to explain his borrowing the family shotgun. He loaded it with buckshot, and, in the pocket of his shirt buttoned his license to "hunt, pursue and kill, to take with traps or other devices."

He remembered that Judge Van Vorst had warned him, before he arrested more spies, to come to him for a warrant. But with an impatient shake of the head Jimmie tossed the recollection from him. After what he had seen he could not possibly be again mistaken. He did not need a warrant. What he had seen was his warrant–plus the shotgun.

As a "pathfinder" should, he planned to take up the trail where he had lost it, but, before he reached Round Hill, he found a warmer trail. Before him, stamped clearly in the road still damp from the rain of the night before, two lines of little arrow-heads pointed the way. They were so fresh that at each twist in the road, lest the car should be just beyond him, Jimmie slackened his steps. After half a mile the scent grew hot. The tracks were deeper, the arrow-heads more clearly cut, and Jimmie broke into a run. Then, the arrow-heads swung suddenly to the right, and in a clearing at the edge of a wood, were lost. But the tires had pressed deep into the grass, and just inside the wood, he found the car. It was empty. Jimmie was drawn two ways. Should he seek the spy on the nearest hilltop, or, until the owner returned, wait by the car?

Between lying in ambush and action, Jimmie preferred action. But, he did not climb the hill nearest the car; he climbed the hill that overlooked that hill.

Flat on the ground, hidden in the goldenrod, he lay motionless. Before him, for fifteen miles stretched hills and tiny valleys. Six miles away to his right rose the stone steeple, and the red roofs of Greenwich. Directly before him were no signs of habitation, only green forests, green fields, gray stone walls, and, where a road ran up-hill, a splash of white, that quivered in the heat. The storm of the night before had washed the air. Each leaf stood by itself. Nothing stirred; and in the glare of the August sun every detail of the landscape was as distinct as those in a colored photograph; and as still.

In his excitement the scout was trembling.

"If he moves," he sighed happily, "I've got him!"

Opposite, across a little valley was the hill at the base of which he had found the car. The slope toward him was bare, but the top was crowned with a thick wood; and along its crest, as though establishing an ancient boundary, ran a stone wall, moss-covered and wrapped in poison-ivy. In places, the branches of the trees, reaching out to the sun, overhung the wall and hid it in black shadows. Jimmie divided the hill into sectors. He began at the right, and slowly followed the wall. With his eyes he took it apart, stone by stone. Had a chipmunk raised his head, Jimmie would have seen him. So, when from the stone wall, like the reflection of the sun upon a window-pane, something flashed, Jimmie knew he had found his spy. A pair of binoculars had betrayed him. Jimmie now saw him clearly. He sat on the ground at the top of the hill opposite, in the deep shadow of an oak, his back against the stone wall. With the binoculars to his eyes he had leaned too far forward, and upon the glass the sun had flashed a warning.

Jimmie appreciated that his attack must be made from the rear. Backward, like a crab he wriggled free of the goldenrod, and hidden by the contour of the hill, raced down it and into the woods on the hill opposite. When he came to within twenty feet of the oak beneath which he had seen the stranger, he stood erect, and as though avoiding a live wire, stepped on tiptoe to the wall. The stranger still sat against it. The binoculars hung from a cord around his neck. Across his knees was spread a map. He was marking it with a pencil, and as he worked he hummed a tune.

Jimmie knelt, and resting the gun on the top of the wall, covered him.

"Throw up your hands!" he commanded.

The stranger did not start. Except that he raised his eyes he gave no sign that he had heard. His eyes stared across the little sun-filled valley. They were half closed as though in study, as though perplexed by some deep and intricate problem. They appeared to see beyond the sun-filled valley some place of greater moment, some place far distant.

Then the eyes smiled, and slowly, as though his neck were stiff, but still smiling, the stranger turned his head. When he saw the boy, his smile was swept away in waves of surprise, amazement, and disbelief. These were followed instantly by an expression of the most acute alarm.

"Don't point that thing at me!" shouted the stranger. "Is it loaded?" With his cheek pressed to the stock and his eye squinted down the length of the brown barrel, Jimmie nodded. The stranger flung up his open palms. They accented his expression of amazed incredulity. He seemed to be exclaiming, "Can such things be?"

"Get up!" commanded Jimmie.

With alacrity the stranger rose.

"Walk over there," ordered the scout. "Walk backward. Stop! Take off those field-glasses and throw them to me." Without removing his eyes from the gun the stranger lifted the binoculars from his neck and tossed them to the stone wall.

"See here!" he pleaded, "if you'll only point that damned blunderbuss the other way, you can have the glasses, and my watch, and clothes, and all my money; only don't—"

Jimmie flushed crimson. "You can't bribe me," he growled. At least, he tried to growl, but because his voice was changing, or because he was excited the growl ended in a high squeak. With mortification, Jimmie flushed a deeper crimson. But the stranger was not amused. At Jimmie's words he seemed rather the more amazed.

"I'm not trying to bribe you," he protested. "If you don't want anything, why are you holding me up?"

"I'm not," returned Jimmie, "I'm arresting you!"

The stranger laughed with relief. Again his eyes smiled. "Oh," he cried, "I see! Have I been trespassing?"

With a glance Jimmie measured the distance between himself and the stranger. Reassured, he lifted one leg after the other over the wall. "If you try to rush me," he warned, "I'll shoot you full of buckshot."

The stranger took a hasty step backward.

"Don't worry about that," he exclaimed. "I'll not rush you. Why am I arrested?"

Hugging the shotgun with his left arm, Jimmie stopped and lifted the binoculars. He gave them a swift glance, slung them over his shoulder, and again clutched his weapon. His expression was now stern and menacing.

"The name on them," he accused, "is 'Weiss, Berlin.' Is that your name?" The stranger smiled, but corrected himself, and replied gravely, "That's the name of the firm that makes them."

Jimmie exclaimed in triumph. "Hah!" he cried, "made in Germany!"

The stranger shook his head.

"I don't understand," he said. "Where would a Weiss glass be made?" With polite insistence he repeated, "Would you mind telling me why I am arrested, and who you might happen to be?"

Jimmie did not answer. Again he stooped and picked up the map, and as he did so, for the first time the face of the stranger showed that he was annoyed. Jimmie was not at home with maps. They told him nothing. But the penciled notes on this one made easy reading. At his first glance he saw, "Correct range, 1,800 yards"; "this stream not fordable"; "slope of hill 15 degrees inaccessible for artillery." "Wire entanglements here"; "forage for five squadrons."

Jimmie's eyes flashed. He shoved the map inside his shirt, and with the gun motioned toward the base of the hill. "Keep forty feet ahead of me," he commanded, "and walk to your car." The stranger did not seem to hear him. He spoke with irritation.

"I suppose," he said, "I'll have to explain to you about that map."

"Not to me, you won't," declared his captor. "You're going to drive straight to Judge Van Vorst's, and explain to him!"

The stranger tossed his arms even higher. "Thank God!" he exclaimed gratefully.

With his prisoner Jimmie encountered no further trouble. He made a willing captive. And if in covering the five miles to Judge Van Vorst's he exceeded the speed limit, the fact that from the rear seat Jimmie held the shotgun against the base of his skull was an extenuating circumstance.

They arrived in the nick of time. In his own car young Van Vorst and a bag of golf clubs were just drawing away from the house. Seeing the car climbing the steep driveway that for a half-mile led from his lodge to his front door, and seeing Jimmie standing in the tonneau brandishing a gun, the Judge hastily descended. The sight of the spy hunter filled him with misgiving, but the sight of him gave Jimmie sweet relief. Arresting German spies for a small boy is no easy task. For Jimmie the strain was great. And now that he knew he had successfully delivered him into the hands of the law, Jimmie's heart rose with happiness. The added presence of a butler of magnificent bearing and of an athletic looking chauffeur increased his sense of security. Their presence seemed to afford a feeling of security to the prisoner also. As he brought the car to a halt, he breathed a sigh. It was a sigh of deep relief.

Jimmie fell from the tonneau. In concealing his sense of triumph, he was not entirely successful.

"I got him!" he cried. "I didn't make no mistake about this one!"

"What one?" demanded Van Vorst.

Jimmie pointed dramatically at his prisoner. With an anxious expression the stranger was tenderly fingering the back of his head. He seemed to wish to assure himself that it was still there.

"That one!" cried Jimmie. "He's a German spy!"

The patience of Judge Van Vorst fell from him. In his exclamation was indignation, anger, reproach.

"Jimmie!" he cried.

Jimmie thrust into his hand the map. It was his "Exhibit A." "Look what he's wrote," commanded the scout. "It's all military words. And these are his glasses. I took 'em off him. They're made in Germany! I been stalking him for a week. He's a spy!"

When Jimmie thrust the map before his face, Van Vorst had glanced at it. Then he regarded it more closely. As he raised his eyes they showed that he was puzzled.

But he greeted the prisoner politely.

"I'm extremely sorry you've been annoyed," he said. "I'm only glad it's no worse. He might have shot you. He's mad over the idea that every stranger he sees—"

The prisoner quickly interrupted.

"Please!" he begged, "don't blame the boy. He behaved extremely well. Might I speak with you–alone?" he asked.

Judge Van Vorst led the way across the terrace, and to the smoking-room, that served also as his office, and closed the door. The stranger walked directly to the mantelpiece and put his finger on a gold cup.

"I saw your mare win that at Belmont Park," he said. "She must have been a great loss to you?"

"She was," said Van Vorst. "The week before she broke her back, I refused three thousand for her. Will you have a cigarette?"

The stranger waved aside the cigarettes.

"I brought you inside," he said, "because I didn't want your servants to hear; and because I don't want to hurt that boy's feelings. He's a fine boy; and he's a damned clever scout. I knew he was following me and I threw him off twice, but to-day he caught me fair. If I really had been a German spy, I couldn't have got away from him. And I want him to think he has captured a German spy. Because he deserves just as much credit as though he had, and because it's best he shouldn't know whom he did capture."

Van Vorst pointed to the map. "My bet is," he said, "that you're an officer of the State militia, taking notes for the fall manœuvres. Am I right?"

The stranger smiled in approval, but shook his head.

"You're warm," he said, "but it's more serious than manœuvres. It's the Real Thing." From his pocketbook he took a visiting card and laid it on the table. "I'm 'Sherry' McCoy," he said, "Captain of Artillery in the United States Army." He nodded to the hand telephone on the table.

"You can call up Governor's Island and get General Wood or his aide, Captain Dorey, on the phone. They sent me here. Ask them. I'm not picking out gun sites for the Germans; I'm picking out positions of defense for Americans when the Germans come!"

Van Vorst laughed derisively.

"My word!" he exclaimed. "You're as bad as Jimmie!"

Captain McCoy regarded him with disfavor.

"And you, sir," he retorted, "are as bad as ninety million other Americans. You won't believe! When the Germans are shelling this hill, when they're taking your hunters to pull their cook-wagons, maybe, you'll believe then."

"Are you serious?" demanded Van Vorst. "And you an army officer?"

"That's why I am serious," returned McCoy. "We know. But when we try to prepare for what is coming, we must do it secretly–in underhand ways, for fear the newspapers will get hold of it and ridicule us, and accuse us of trying to drag the country into war. That's why we have to prepare under cover. That's why I've had to skulk around these hills like a chicken thief. And," he added sharply, "that's why that boy must not know who I am. If he does, the General Staff will get a calling down at Washington, and I'll have my ears boxed."

Van Vorst moved to the door.

"He will never learn the truth from me," he said. "For I will tell him you are to be shot at sunrise."

"Good!" laughed the Captain. "And tell me his name. If ever we fight over Westchester County, I want that lad for my chief of scouts. And give him this. Tell him to buy a new scout uniform. Tell him it comes from you."

But no money could reconcile Jimmie to the sentence imposed upon his captive. He received the news with a howl of anguish. "You mustn't," he begged; "I never knowed you'd shoot him! I wouldn't have caught him if I'd knowed that. I couldn't sleep if I thought he was going to be shot at sunrise." At the prospect of unending nightmares Jimmie's voice shook with terror. "Make it for twenty years," he begged. "Make it for ten," he coaxed, "but, please, promise you won't shoot him."

When Van Vorst returned to Captain McCoy, he was smiling, and the butler who followed, bearing a tray and tinkling glasses, was trying not to smile.

"I gave Jimmie your ten dollars," said Van Vorst, "and made it twenty, and he has gone home. You will be glad to hear that he begged me to spare your life, and that your sentence has been commuted to twenty years in a fortress. I drink to your good fortune."

"No!" protested Captain McCoy, "we will drink to Jimmie!"

When Captain McCoy had driven away, and his own car and the golf clubs had again been brought to the steps, Judge Van Vorst once more attempted to depart; but he was again delayed.

Other visitors were arriving.

Up the driveway a touring-car approached, and though it limped on a flat tire, it approached at reckless speed. The two men in the front seat were white with dust; their faces, masked by automobile glasses, were indistinguishable. As though preparing for an immediate exit, the car swung in a circle until its nose pointed down the driveway up which it had just come. Raising his silk mask the one beside the driver shouted at Judge Van Vorst. His throat was parched, his voice was hoarse and hot with anger.

"A gray touring-car," he shouted. "It stopped here. We saw it from that hill. Then the damn tire burst, and we lost our way. Where did he go?"

"Who?" demanded Van Vorst, stiffly, "Captain McCoy?"

The man exploded with an oath. The driver, with a shove of his elbow, silenced him.

"Yes, Captain McCoy," assented the driver eagerly. "Which way did he go?"

"To New York," said Van Vorst.

The driver shrieked at his companion.

"Then, he's doubled back," he cried. "He's gone to New Haven." He stooped and threw in the clutch. The car lurched forward.

A cold terror swept young Van Vorst.

"What do you want with him?" he called. "Who are you?"

Over one shoulder the masked face glared at him. Above the roar of the car the words of the driver were flung back.

"We're Secret Service from Washington," he shouted. "He's from their embassy. He's a German spy!"

Leaping and throbbing at sixty miles an hour, the car vanished in a curtain of white, whirling dust.

GALLEGHER

A NEWSPAPER STORY

We had had so many office-boys before Gallegher came among us that they had begun to lose the characteristics of individuals, and became merged in a composite photograph of small boys, to whom we applied the generic title of "Here, you"; or "You, boy."

We had had sleepy boys, and lazy boys, and bright, "smart" boys, who became so familiar on so short an acquaintance that we were forced to part with them to save our own self-respect.

They generally graduated into district-messenger boys, and occasionally returned to us in blue coats with nickel-plated buttons, and patronized us.

But Gallegher was something different from anything we had experienced before. Gallegher was short and broad in build, with a solid, muscular broadness, and not a fat and dumpy shortness. He wore perpetually on his face a happy and knowing smile, as if you and the world in general were not impressing him as seriously as you thought you were, and his eyes, which were very black and very bright, snapped intelligently at you like those of a little black-and-tan terrier.

All Gallegher knew had been learnt on the streets; not a very good school in itself, but one that turns out very knowing scholars. And Gallegher had attended both morning and evening sessions. He could not tell you who the Pilgrim Fathers were, nor could he name the thirteen original States, but he knew all the officers of the twenty-second police district by name, and he could distinguish the clang of a fire-engine's gong from that of a patrol-wagon or an ambulance fully two blocks distant. It was Gallegher who rang the alarm when the Woolwich Mills caught fire, while the officer on the beat was asleep, and it was Gallegher who led the "Black Diamonds" against the "Wharf Rats," when they used to stone each other to their heart's content on the coal-wharves of Richmond.

I am afraid, now that I see these facts written down, that Gallegher was not a reputable character; but he was so very young and so very old for his years that we all liked him very much nevertheless. He lived in the extreme northern part of Philadelphia, where the cotton and woollen mills run down to the river, and how he ever got home after leaving the Press building at two in the morning, was one of the mysteries of the office. Sometimes he caught a night car, and sometimes he walked all the way, arriving at the little house, where his mother and himself lived alone, at four in the morning. Occasionally he was given a ride on an early milk-cart, or on one of the newspaper delivery wagons, with its high piles of papers still damp and sticky from the press. He knew several drivers of "night hawks"–those cabs that prowl the streets at night looking for belated passengers–and when it was a very cold morning he would not go home at all, but would crawl into one of these cabs and sleep, curled up on the cushions, until daylight.

Besides being quick and cheerful, Gallegher possessed a power of amusing the Press's young men to a degree seldom attained by the ordinary mortal. His clog-dancing on the city editor's desk, when that gentleman was up-stairs fighting for two more columns of space, was always a source of innocent joy to us, and his imitations of the comedians of the variety halls delighted even the dramatic critic, from whom the comedians themselves failed to force a smile.

But Gallegher's chief characteristic was his love for that element of news generically classed as "crime."

Not that he ever did anything criminal himself. On the contrary, his was rather the work of the criminal specialist, and his morbid interest in the doings of all queer characters, his knowledge of their methods, their present whereabouts, and their past deeds of transgression often rendered him a valuable ally to our police reporter, whose daily feuilletons were the only portion of the paper Gallegher deigned to read.

In Gallegher the detective element was abnormally developed. He had shown this on several occasions, and to excellent purpose.

Once the paper had sent him into a Home for Destitute Orphans which was believed to be grievously mismanaged, and Gallegher, while playing the part of a destitute orphan, kept his eyes open to what was going on around him so faithfully that the story he told of the treatment meted out to the real orphans was sufficient to rescue the unhappy little wretches from the individual who had them in charge, and to have the individual himself sent to jail.

Gallegher's knowledge of the aliases, terms of imprisonment, and various misdoings of the leading criminals in Philadelphia was almost as thorough as that of the chief of police himself, and he could tell to an hour when "Dutchy Mack" was to be let out of prison, and could identify at a glance "Dick Oxford, confidence man," as "Gentleman Dan, petty thief."

There were, at this time, only two pieces of news in any of the papers. The least important of the two was the big fight between the Champion of the United States and the Would-be Champion, arranged to take place near Philadelphia; the second was the Burrbank murder, which was filling space in newspapers all over the world, from New York to Bombay.

Richard F. Burrbank was one of the most prominent of New York's railroad lawyers; he was also, as a matter of course, an owner of much railroad stock, and a very wealthy man. He had been spoken of as a political possibility for many high offices, and, as the counsel for a great railroad, was known even further than the great railroad itself had stretched its system.

At six o'clock one morning he was found by his butler lying at the foot of the hall stairs with two pistol wounds above his heart. He was quite dead. His safe, to which only he and his secretary had the keys, was found open, and $200,000 in bonds, stocks, and money, which had been placed there only the night before, was found missing. The secretary was missing also. His name was Stephen S. Hade, and his name and his description had been telegraphed and cabled to all parts of the world. There was enough circumstantial evidence to show, beyond any question or possibility of mistake, that he was the murderer.

It made an enormous amount of talk, and unhappy individuals were being arrested all over the country, and sent on to New York for identification. Three had been arrested at Liverpool, and one man just as he landed at Sydney, Australia. But so far the murderer had escaped.

We were all talking about it one night, as everybody else was all over the country, in the local room, and the city editor said it was worth a fortune to any one who chanced to run across Hade and succeeded in handing him over to the police. Some of us thought Hade had taken passage from some one of the smaller seaports, and others were of the opinion that he had buried himself in some cheap lodging-house in New York, or in one of the smaller towns in New Jersey.

"I shouldn't be surprised to meet him out walking, right here in Philadelphia," said one of the staff. "He'll be disguised, of course, but you could always tell him by the absence of the trigger finger on his right hand. It's missing, you know; shot off when he was a boy."

"You want to look for a man dressed like a tough," said the city editor; "for as this fellow is to all appearances a gentleman, he will try to look as little like a gentleman as possible."

"No, he won't," said Gallegher, with that calm impertinence that made him dear to us. "He'll dress just like a gentleman. Toughs don't wear gloves, and you see he's got to wear 'em. The first thing he thought of after doing for Burrbank was of that gone finger, and how he was to hide it. He stuffed the finger of that glove with cotton so's to make it look like a whole finger, and the first time he takes off that glove they've got him—see, and he knows it. So what youse want to do is to look for a man with gloves on. I've been a-doing it for two weeks now, and I can tell you it's hard work, for everybody wears gloves this kind of weather. But if you look long enough you'll find him. And when you think it's him, go up to him and hold out your hand in a friendly way, like a bunco-steerer, and shake his hand; and if you feel that his forefinger ain't real flesh, but just wadded cotton, then grip to it with your right and grab his throat with your left, and holler for help."

There was an appreciative pause.

"I see, gentlemen," said the city editor, dryly, "that Gallegher's reasoning has impressed you; and I also see that before the week is out all of my young men will be under bonds for assaulting innocent pedestrians whose only offense is that they wear gloves in midwinter."

It was about a week after this that Detective Hefflefinger, of Inspector Byrnes's staff, came over to Philadelphia after a burglar, of whose whereabouts he had been misinformed by telegraph. He brought the warrant, requisition, and other necessary papers with him, but the burglar had flown. One of our reporters had worked on a New York paper, and knew Hefflefinger, and the detective came to the office to see if he could help him in his so far unsuccessful search.

He gave Gallegher his card, and after Gallegher had read it, and had discovered who the visitor was, he became so demoralized that he was absolutely useless.

"One of Byrnes's men" was a much more awe-inspiring individual to Gallegher than a member of the Cabinet. He accordingly seized his hat and overcoat, and leaving his duties to be looked after by others, hastened out after the object of his admiration, who found his suggestions and knowledge of the city so valuable, and his company so entertaining, that they became very intimate, and spent the rest of the day together.

In the meanwhile the managing editor had instructed his subordinates to inform Gallegher, when he condescended to return, that his services were no longer needed. Gallegher had played truant once too often. Unconscious of this, he remained with his new friend until late the same evening, and started the next afternoon toward the Press office.

As I have said, Gallegher lived in the most distant part of the city, not many minutes' walk from the Kensington railroad station, where trains ran into the suburbs and on to New York.

It was in front of this station that a smoothly shaven, well-dressed man brushed past Gallegher and hurried up the steps to the ticket office.

He held a walking-stick in his right hand, and Gallegher, who now patiently scrutinized the hands of every one who wore gloves, saw that while three fingers of the man's hand were closed around the cane, the fourth stood out in almost a straight line with his palm.

Gallegher stopped with a gasp and with a trembling all over his little body, and his brain asked with a throb if it could be possible. But possibilities and probabilities were to be discovered later. Now was the time for action.

He was after the man in a moment, hanging at his heels and his eyes moist with excitement.

He heard the man ask for a ticket to Torresdale, a little station just outside of Philadelphia, and when he was out of hearing, but not out of sight, purchased one for the same place.

The stranger went into the smoking-car, and seated himself at one end toward the door. Gallegher took his place at the opposite end.

He was trembling all over, and suffered from a slight feeling of nausea. He guessed it came from fright, not of any bodily harm that might come to him, but of the probability of failure in his adventure and of its most momentous possibilities.

The stranger pulled his coat collar up around his ears, hiding the lower portion of his face, but not concealing the resemblance in his troubled eyes and close-shut lips to the likenesses of the murderer Hade.

They reached Torresdale in half an hour, and the stranger, alighting quickly, struck off at a rapid pace down the country road leading to the station.

Gallegher gave him a hundred yards' start, and then followed slowly after. The road ran between fields and past a few frame-houses set far from the road in kitchen gardens.

Once or twice the man looked back over his shoulder, but he saw only a dreary length of road with a small boy splashing through the slush in the midst of it and stopping every now and again to throw snowballs at belated sparrows.

After a ten minutes' walk the stranger turned into a side road which led to only one place, the Eagle Inn, an old roadside hostelry known now as the headquarters for pothunters from the Philadelphia game market and the battleground of many a cock-fight.

Gallegher knew the place well. He and his young companions had often stopped there when out chestnutting on holidays in the autumn.

The son of the man who kept it had often accompanied them on their excursions, and though the boys of the city streets considered him a dumb lout, they respected him somewhat owing to his inside knowledge of dog and cock-fights.

The stranger entered the inn at a side door, and Gallegher, reaching it a few minutes later, let him go for the time being, and set about finding his occasional playmate, young Keppler.

Keppler's offspring was found in the woodshed.

"Tain't hard to guess what brings you out here," said the tavern-keeper's son, with a grin; "it's the fight."

"What fight?" asked Gallegher, unguardedly.

"What fight? Why, the fight," returned his companion, with the slow contempt of superior knowledge. "It's to come off here to-night. You knew that as well as me; anyway your sportin' editor knows it. He got the tip last night, but that won't help you any. You needn't think there's any chance of your getting a peep at it. Why, tickets is two hundred and fifty apiece!"

"Whew!" whistled Gallegher, "where's it to be?"

"In the barn," whispered Keppler. "I helped 'em fix the ropes this morning, I did."

"Gosh, but you're in luck," exclaimed Gallegher, with flattering envy. "Couldn't I jest get a peep at it?"

"Maybe," said the gratified Keppler. "There's a winder with a wooden shutter at the back of the barn. You can get in by it, if you have some one to boost you up to the sill."

"Sa-a-y," drawled Gallegher, as if something had but just that moment reminded him. "Who's that gent who come down the road just a bit ahead of me—him with the cape-coat! Has he got anything to do with the fight?"

"Him?" repeated Keppler in tones of sincere disgust. "No-oh, he ain't no sport. He's queer, Dad thinks. He come here one day last week about ten in the morning, said his doctor told him to go out 'en the country for his health. He's stuck up and citified, and wears gloves, and takes his meals private in his room, and all that sort of ruck. They was saying in the saloon last night that they thought he was hiding from something, and Dad, just to try him, asks him last night if he was coming to see the fight. He looked sort of scared, and said he didn't want to see no fight. And then Dad says, 'I guess you mean you don't want no fighters to see you.' Dad didn't mean no harm by it, just passed it as a joke; but Mr. Carleton, as he calls himself, got white as a ghost an' says, 'I'll go to the fight willing enough,' and begins to laugh and joke. And this morning he went right into the bar-room, where all the sports were setting, and said he was going into town to see some friends; and as he starts off he laughs an' says, 'This don't look as if I was afraid of seeing people, does it?' but Dad says it was just bluff that made him do it, and Dad thinks that if he hadn't said what he did, this Mr. Carleton wouldn't have left his room at all."

Gallegher had got all he wanted, and much more than he had hoped for–so much more that his walk back to the station was in the nature of a triumphal march.

He had twenty minutes to wait for the next train, and it seemed an hour. While waiting he sent a telegram to Hefflefinger at his hotel. It read:

Your man is near the Torresdale station, on Pennsylvania Railroad; take cab, and meet me at station. Wait until I come.

Gallegher.

With the exception of one at midnight, no other train stopped at Torresdale that evening, hence the direction to take a cab.

The train to the city seemed to Gallegher to drag itself by inches. It stopped and backed at purposeless intervals, waited for an express to precede it, and dallied at stations, and when, at last, it reached the terminus, Gallegher was out before it had stopped and was in the cab and off on his way to the home of the sporting editor.

The sporting editor was at dinner and came out in the hall to see him, with his napkin in his hand. Gallegher explained breathlessly that he had located the murderer for whom the police of two continents were looking, and that he believed, in order to quiet the suspicions of the people with whom he was hiding, that he would be present at the fight that night.

The sporting editor led Gallegher into his library and shut the door. "Now," he said, "go over all that again."

Gallegher went over it again in detail, and added how he had sent for Hefflefinger to make the arrest in order that it might be kept from the knowledge of the local police and from the Philadelphia reporters.

"What I want Hefflefinger to do is to arrest Hade with the warrant he has for the burglar," explained Gallegher; "and to take him on to New York on the owl train that passes Torresdale at one. It don't get to Jersey City until four o'clock, one hour after the morning papers go to press. Of course, we must fix Hefflefinger so's he'll keep quiet and not tell who his prisoner really is."

The sporting editor reached his hand out to pat Gallegher on the head, but changed his mind and shook hands with him instead.

"My boy," he said, "you are an infant phenomenon. If I can pull the rest of this thing off to-night it will mean the $5,000 reward and fame galore for you and the paper. Now, I'm going to write a note to the managing editor, and you can take it around to him and tell him what you've done and what I am going to do, and he'll take you back on the paper and raise your salary. Perhaps you didn't know you've been discharged?"

"Do you think you ain't a-going to take me with you?" demanded Gallegher.

"Why, certainly not. Why should I? It all lies with the detective and myself now. You've done your share, and done it well. If the man's caught, the reward's yours. But you'd only be in the way now. You'd better go to the office and make your peace with the chief."

"If the paper can get along without me, I can get along without the old paper," said Gallegher, hotly. "And if I ain't a-going with you, you ain't neither, for I know where Hefflefinger is to be, and you don't, and I won't tell you."

"Oh, very well, very well," replied the sporting editor, weakly capitulating. "I'll send the note by a messenger; only mind, if you lose your place, don't blame me."

Gallegher wondered how this man could value a week's salary against the excitement of seeing a noted criminal run down, and of getting the news to the paper, and to that one paper alone.

From that moment the sporting editor sank in Gallegher's estimation.

Mr. Dwyer sat down at his desk and scribbled off the following note:

I have received reliable information that Hade, the Burrbank murderer, will be present at the fight to-night. We have arranged it so that he will be arrested quietly and in such a manner that the fact may be kept from all other papers. I need not point out to you that this will be the most important piece of news in the country to-morrow. Yours, etc.,

Michael E. Dwyer.

The sporting editor stepped into the waiting cab, while Gallegher whispered the directions to the driver. He was told to go first to a district-messenger office, and from there up to the Ridge Avenue Road, out Broad Street, and on to the old Eagle Inn, near Torresdale.

It was a miserable night. The rain and snow were falling together, and freezing as they fell. The sporting editor got out to send his message to the Press office, and then lighting a cigar, and turning up the collar of his great-coat, curled up in the corner of the cab.

"Wake me when we get there, Gallegher," he said. He knew he had a long ride, and much rapid work before him, and he was preparing for the strain.

To Gallegher the idea of going to sleep seemed almost criminal. From the dark corner of the cab his eyes shone with excitement, and with the awful joy of anticipation. He glanced every now and then to where the sporting editor's cigar shone in the darkness, and watched it as it gradually burnt more dimly and went out. The lights in the shop windows threw a broad glare across the ice on the pavements, and the lights from the lamp-posts tossed the distorted shadow of the cab, and the horse, and the motionless driver, sometimes before and sometimes behind them.

After half an hour Gallegher slipped down to the bottom of the cab and dragged out a lap-robe, in which he wrapped himself. It was growing colder, and the damp, keen wind swept in through the cracks until the window-frames and woodwork were cold to the touch.

An hour passed, and the cab was still moving more slowly over the rough surface of partly paved streets, and by single rows of new houses standing at different angles to each other in fields covered with ash-heaps and brick-kilns. Here and there the gaudy lights of a drug-store, and the forerunner of suburban civilization, shone from the end of a new block of houses, and the rubber cape of an occasional policeman showed in the light of the lamp-post that he hugged for comfort.

Then even the houses disappeared, and the cab dragged its way between truck farms, with desolate-looking glass-covered beds, and pools of water, half-caked with ice, and bare trees, and interminable fences.

Once or twice the cab stopped altogether, and Gallegher could hear the driver swearing to himself, or at the horse, or the roads. At last they drew up before the station at Torresdale. It was quite deserted, and only a single light cut a swath in the darkness and showed a portion of the platform, the ties, and the rails glistening in the rain. They walked twice past the light before a figure stepped out of the shadow and greeted them cautiously.

"I am Mr. Dwyer, of the Press," said the sporting editor, briskly. "You've heard of me, perhaps. Well, there shouldn't be any difficulty in our making a deal, should there? This boy here has found Hade, and we have reason to believe he will be among the spectators at the fight to-night. We want you to arrest him quietly, and as secretly as possible. You can do it with your papers and your badge easily enough. We want you to pretend that you believe he is this burglar you came over after. If you will do this, and take him away without any one so much as suspecting who he really is, and on the train that passes here at 1.20 for New York, we will give you $500 out of the $5,000 reward. If, however, one other paper, either in New York or Philadelphia, or anywhere else, knows of the arrest, you won't get a cent. Now, what do you say?"

The detective had a great deal to say. He wasn't at all sure the man Gallegher suspected was Hade; he feared he might get himself into trouble by making a false arrest, and if it should be the man, he was afraid the local police would interfere.

"We've no time to argue or debate this matter," said Dwyer, warmly. "We agree to point Hade out to you in the crowd. After the fight is over you arrest him as we have directed, and you get the money and the credit of the arrest. If you don't like this, I will arrest the man myself, and have him driven to town, with a pistol for a warrant."

Hefflefinger considered in silence and then agreed unconditionally. "As you say, Mr. Dwyer," he returned. "I've heard of you for a thoroughbred sport. I know you'll do what you say you'll do; and as for me I'll do what you say and just as you say, and it's a very pretty piece of work as it stands."

They all stepped back into the cab, and then it was that they were met by a fresh difficulty, how to get the detective into the barn where the fight was to take place, for neither of the two men had $250 to pay for his admittance.

But this was overcome when Gallegher remembered the window of which young Keppler had told him.

In the event of Hade's losing courage and not daring to show himself in the crowd around the ring, it was agreed that Dwyer should come to the barn and warn Hefflefinger; but if he should come, Dwyer was merely to keep near him and to signify by a prearranged gesture which one of the crowd he was.

They drew up before a great black shadow of a house, dark, forbidding, and apparently deserted. But at the sound of the wheels on the gravel the door opened, letting out a stream of warm, cheerful light, and a man's voice said, "Put out those lights. Don't youse know no better than that?" This was Keppler, and he welcomed Mr. Dwyer with effusive courtesy.

The two men showed in the stream of light, and the door closed on them, leaving the house as it was at first, black and silent, save for the dripping of the rain and snow from the eaves.

The detective and Gallegher put out the cab's lamps and led the horse toward a long, low shed in the rear of the yard, which they now noticed was almost filled with teams of many different makes, from the Hobson's choice of a livery stable to the brougham of the man about town.

"No," said Gallegher, as the cabman stopped to hitch the horse beside the others, "we want it nearest that lower gate. When we newspaper men leave this place we'll leave it in a hurry, and the man who is nearest town is likely to get there first. You won't be a-following of no hearse when you make your return trip."

Gallegher tied the horse to the very gate-post itself, leaving the gate open and allowing a clear road and a flying start for the prospective race to Newspaper Row.

The driver disappeared under the shelter of the porch, and Gallegher and the detective moved off cautiously to the rear of the barn. "This must be the window," said Hefflefinger, pointing to a broad wooden shutter some feet from the ground.

"Just you give me a boost once, and I'll get that open in a jiffy," said Gallegher.

The detective placed his hands on his knees, and Gallegher stood upon his shoulders, and with the blade of his knife lifted the wooden button that fastened the window on the inside, and pulled the shutter open.

Then he put one leg inside over the sill, and leaning down helped to draw his fellow-conspirator up to a level with the window. "I feel just like I was burglarizing a house," chuckled Gallegher, as he dropped noiselessly to the floor below and refastened the shutter. The barn was a large one, with a row of stalls on either side in which horses and cows were dozing. There was a haymow over each row of stalls, and at one end of the barn a number of fence-rails had been thrown across from one mow to the other. These rails were covered with hay.

In the middle of the floor was the ring. It was not really a ring, but a square, with wooden posts at its four corners through which ran a heavy rope. The space enclosed by the rope was covered with sawdust.

Gallegher could not resist stepping into the ring, and after stamping the sawdust once or twice, as if to assure himself that he was really there, began dancing around it, and indulging in such a remarkable series of fistic manœuvres with an imaginary adversary that the unimaginative detective precipitately backed into a corner of the barn.

"Now, then," said Gallegher, having apparently vanquished his foe, "you come with me." His companion followed quickly as Gallegher climbed to one of the hay-mows, and, crawling carefully out on the fence-rail, stretched himself at full length, face downward. In this position, by moving the straw a little, he could look down, without being himself seen, upon the heads of whomsoever stood below. "This is better'n a private box, ain't it?" said Gallegher.

The boy from the newspaper office and the detective lay there in silence, biting at straws and tossing anxiously on their comfortable bed.

It seemed fully two hours before they came. Gallegher had listened without breathing, and with every muscle on a strain, at least a dozen times, when some movement in the yard had led him to believe that they were at the door.

And he had numerous doubts and fears. Sometimes it was that the police had learnt of the fight, and had raided Keppler's in his absence, and again it was that the fight had been postponed, or, worst of all, that it would be put off until so late that Mr. Dwyer could not get back in time for the last edition of the paper. Their coming, when at last they came, was heralded by an advance-guard of two sporting men, who stationed themselves at either side of the big door.

"Hurry up, now, gents," one of the men said with a shiver, "don't keep this door open no longer'n is needful."

It was not a very large crowd, but it was wonderfully well selected. It ran, in the majority of its component parts, to heavy white coats with pearl buttons. The white coats were shouldered by long blue coats with astrakhan fur trimmings, the wearers of which preserved a cliqueness not remarkable when one considers that they believed every one else present to be either a crook or a prize-fighter.

There were well-fed, well-groomed club-men and brokers in the crowd, a politician or two, a popular comedian with his manager, amateur boxers from the athletic clubs, and quiet, close-mouthed sporting men from every city in the country. Their names if printed in the papers would have been as familiar as the types of the papers themselves.

And among these men, whose only thought was of the brutal sport to come, was Hade, with Dwyer standing at ease at his shoulder–Hade, white, and visibly in deep anxiety, hiding his pale face beneath a cloth travelling-cap, and with his chin muffled in a woollen scarf. He had dared to come because he feared his danger from the already suspicious Keppler was less than if he stayed away. And so he was there, hovering restlessly on the border of the crowd, feeling his danger and sick with fear.

When Hefflefinger first saw him he started up on his hands and elbows and made a movement forward as if he would leap down then and there and carry off his prisoner single-handed.

"Lie down," growled Gallegher; "an officer of any sort wouldn't live three minutes in that crowd."

The detective drew back slowly and buried himself again in the straw, but never once through the long fight which followed did his eyes leave the person of the murderer. The newspaper men took their places in the foremost row close around the ring, and kept looking at their watches and begging the master of ceremonies to "shake it up, do."

There was a great deal of betting, and all of the men handled the great rolls of bills they wagered with a flippant recklessness which could only be accounted for in Gallegher's mind by temporary mental derangement. Some one pulled a box out into the ring and the master of ceremonies mounted it, and pointed out in forcible language that as they were almost all already under bonds to keep the peace, it behooved all to curb their excitement and to maintain a severe silence, unless they wanted to bring the police upon them and have themselves "sent down" for a year or two.

Then two very disreputable-looking persons tossed their respective principals' high hats into the ring, and the crowd, recognizing in this relic of the days when brave knights threw down their gauntlets in the lists as only a sign that the fight was about to begin, cheered tumultuously.

This was followed by a sudden surging forward, and a mutter of admiration much more flattering than the cheers had been, when the principals followed their hats and, slipping out of their great-coats, stood forth in all the physical beauty of the perfect brute.

Their pink skin was as soft and healthy-looking as a baby's, and glowed in the lights of the lanterns like tinted ivory, and underneath this silken covering the great biceps and muscles moved in and out and looked like the coils of a snake around the branch of a tree.

Gentleman and blackguard shouldered each other for a nearer view; the coachmen, whose metal buttons were unpleasantly suggestive of police, put their hands, in the excitement of the moment, on the shoulders of their masters; the perspiration stood out in great drops on the foreheads of the backers, and the newspaper men bit somewhat nervously at the ends of their pencils.

And in the stalls the cows munched contentedly at their cuds and gazed with gentle curiosity at their two fellow-brutes, who stood waiting the signal to fall upon and kill each other, if need be, for the delectation of their brothers.

"Take your places," commanded the master of ceremonies.

In the moment in which the two men faced each other the crowd became so still that, save for the beating of the rain upon the shingled roof and the stamping of a horse in one of the stalls, the place was as silent as a church.

"Time," shouted the master of ceremonies.

The two men sprang into a posture of defense, which was lost as quickly as it was taken, one great arm shot out like a piston-rod; there was the sound of bare fists beating on naked flesh; there was an exultant indrawn gasp of savage pleasure and relief from the crowd, and the great fight had begun.

How the fortunes of war rose and fell, and changed and rechanged that night, is an old story to those who listen to such stories; and those who do not will be glad to be spared the telling of it. It was, they say, one of the bitterest fights between two men that this country has ever known.

But all that is of interest here is that after an hour of this desperate, brutal business the champion ceased to be the favorite; the man whom he had taunted and bullied, and for whom the public had but little sympathy, was proving himself a likely winner, and under his cruel blows, as sharp and clean as those from a cutlass, his opponent was rapidly giving way.

The men about the ropes were past all control now; they drowned Keppler's petitions for silence with oaths and in inarticulate shouts of anger, as if the blows had fallen upon them, and in mad rejoicings. They swept from one end of the ring to the other, with every muscle leaping in unison with those of the man they favored, and when a New York correspondent muttered over his shoulder that this would be the biggest sporting surprise since the Heenan-Sayers fight, Mr. Dwyer nodded his head sympathetically in assent.

In the excitement and tumult it is doubtful if any heard the three quickly repeated blows that fell heavily from the outside upon the big doors of the barn. If they did, it was already too late to mend matters, for the door fell, torn from its hinges, and as it fell a captain of police sprang into the light from out of the storm, with his lieutenants and their men crowding close at his shoulder.

In the panic and stampede that followed, several of the men stood as helplessly immovable as though they had seen a ghost; others made a mad rush into the arms of the officers and were beaten back against the ropes of the ring; others dived headlong into the stalls, among the horses and cattle, and still others shoved the rolls of money they held into the hands of the police and begged like children to be allowed to escape.

The instant the door fell and the raid was declared Hefflefinger slipped over the cross rails on which he had been lying, hung for an instant by his hands, and then dropped into the centre of the fighting mob on the floor. He was out of it in an instant with the agility of a pickpocket, was across the room and at Hade's throat like a dog. The murderer, for the moment, was the calmer man of the two.

"Here," he panted, "hands off, now. There's no need for all this violence. There's no great harm in looking at a fight, is there? There's a hundred-dollar bill in my right hand; take it and let me slip out of this. No one is looking. Here."

But the detective only held him the closer.

"I want you for burglary," he whispered under his breath. "You've got to come with me now, and quick. The less fuss you make, the better for both of us. If you don't know who I am, you can feel my badge under my coat there. I've got the authority. It's all regular, and when we're out of this d–d row I'll show you the papers."

He took one hand from Hade's throat and pulled a pair of handcuffs from his pocket.

"It's a mistake. This is an outrage," gasped the murderer, white and trembling, but dreadfully alive and desperate for his liberty. "Let me go, I tell you! Take your hands off of me! Do I look like a burglar, you fool?"

"I know who you look like," whispered the detective, with his face close to the face of his prisoner. "Now, will you go easy as a burglar, or shall I tell these men who you are and what I do want you for? Shall I call out your real name or not? Shall I tell them? Quick, speak up; shall I?"

There was something so exultant–something so unnecessarily savage in the officer's face that the man he held saw that the detective knew him for what he really was, and the hands that had held his throat slipped down around his shoulders, or he would have fallen. The man's eyes opened and closed again, and he swayed weakly backward and forward, and choked as if his throat were dry and burning. Even to such a hardened connoisseur in crime as Gallegher, who stood closely by, drinking it in, there was something so abject in the man's terror that he regarded him with what was almost a touch of pity.

"For God's sake," Hade begged, "let me go. Come with me to my room and I'll give you half the money. I'll divide with you fairly. We can both get away. There's a fortune for both of us there. We both can get away. You'll be rich for life. Do you understand–for life!"

But the detective, to his credit, only shut his lips the tighter.

"That's enough," he whispered, in return. "That's more than I expected. You've sentenced yourself already. Come!"

Two officers in uniform barred their exit at the door, but Hefflefinger smiled easily and showed his badge.

"For God's sake," Hade begged, "let me go."

"One of Byrnes's men," he said, in explanation; "came over expressly to take this chap. He's a burglar; 'Arlie' Lane, alias Carleton. I've shown the papers to the captain. It's all regular. I'm just going to get his traps at the hotel and walk him over to the station. I guess we'll push right on to New York to-night."

The officers nodded and smiled their admiration for the representative of what is, perhaps, the best detective force in the world, and let him pass.

Then Hefflefinger turned and spoke to Gallegher, who still stood as watchful as a dog at his side. "I'm going to his room to get the bonds and stuff," he whispered; "then I'll march him to the station and take that train. I've done my share; don't forget yours!"

"Oh, you'll get your money right enough," said Gallegher. "And, sa-ay," he added, with the appreciative nod of an expert, "do you know, you did it rather well."

Mr. Dwyer had been writing while the raid was settling down, as he had been writing while waiting for the fight to begin. Now he walked over to where the other correspondents stood in angry conclave.

The newspaper men had informed the officers who hemmed them in that they represented the principal papers of the country, and were expostulating vigorously with the captain, who had planned the raid, and who declared they were under arrest.

"Don't be an ass, Scott," said Mr. Dwyer, who was too excited to be polite or politic. "You know our being here isn't a matter of choice. We came here on business, as you did, and you've no right to hold us."

"If we don't get our stuff on the wire at once," protested a New York man, "we'll be too late for to-morrow's paper, and—"

Captain Scott said he did not care a profanely small amount for to-morrow's paper, and that all he knew was that to the station-house the newspaper men would go. There they would have a hearing, and if the magistrate chose to let them off, that was the magistrate's business, but that his duty was to take them into custody.

"But then it will be too late, don't you understand?" shouted Mr. Dwyer. "You've got to let us go now, at once."

"I can't do it, Mr. Dwyer," said the captain, "and that's all there is to it. Why, haven't I just sent the president of the Junior Republican Club to the patrol-wagon, the man that put this coat on me, and do you think I can let you fellows go after that? You were all put under bonds to keep the peace not three days ago, and here you're at it–fighting like badgers. It's worth my place to let one of you off."

What Mr. Dwyer said next was so uncomplimentary to the gallant Captain Scott that that overwrought individual seized the sporting editor by the shoulder, and shoved him into the hands of two of his men.

This was more than the distinguished Mr. Dwyer could brook, and he excitedly raised his hand in resistance. But before he had time to do anything foolish his wrist was gripped by one strong little hand, and he was conscious that another was picking the pocket of his great-coat.

He slapped his hands to his sides, and, looking down, saw Gallegher standing close behind him and holding him by the wrist. Mr. Dwyer had forgotten the boy's existence, and would have spoken sharply if something in Gallegher's innocent eyes had not stopped him.

Gallegher's hand was still in that pocket in which Mr. Dwyer had shoved his notebook filled with what he had written of Gallegher's work and Hade's final capture, and with a running descriptive account of the fight. With his eyes fixed on Mr. Dwyer, Gallegher drew it out, and with a quick movement shoved it inside his waistcoat. Mr. Dwyer gave a nod of comprehension. Then glancing at his two guardsmen, and finding that they were still interested in the wordy battle of the correspondents with their chief, and had seen nothing, he stooped and whispered to Gallegher: "The forms are locked at twenty minutes to three. If you don't get there by that time it will be of no use, but if you're on time you'll beat the town–and the country too."

Gallegher's eyes flashed significantly, and, nodding his head to show he understood, started boldly on a run toward the door. But the officers who guarded it brought him to an abrupt halt, and, much to Mr. Dwyer's astonishment, drew from him what was apparently a torrent of tears.

"Let me go to me father. I want me father," the boy shrieked hysterically. "They've 'rested father. Oh, daddy, daddy. They're a-goin' to take you to prison."

"Who is your father, sonny?" asked one of the guardians of the gate.

"Keppler's me father," sobbed Gallegher. "They're a-goin' to lock him up, and I'll never see him no more."

"Oh, yes, you will," said the officer, good-naturedly; "he's there in that first patrol-wagon. You can run over and say good night to him, and then you'd better get to bed. This ain't no place for kids of your age."

"Thank you, sir," sniffed Gallegher, tearfully, as the two officers raised their clubs, and let him pass out into the darkness.

The yard outside was in a tumult, horses were stamping, and plunging, and backing the carriages into one another; lights were flashing from every window of what had been apparently an uninhabited house, and the voices of the prisoners were still raised in angry expostulation.

Three police patrol-wagons were moving about the yard, filled with unwilling passengers, who sat or stood, packed together like sheep and with no protection from the sleet and rain.

Gallegher stole off into a dark corner, and watched the scene until his eyesight became familiar with the position of the land.

Then with his eyes fixed fearfully on the swinging light of a lantern with which an officer was searching among the carriages, he groped his way between horses' hoofs and behind the wheels of carriages to the cab which he had himself placed at the furthermost gate. It was still there, and the horse, as he had left it, with its head turned toward the city. Gallegher opened the big gate noiselessly, and worked nervously at the hitching strap. The knot was covered with a thin coating of ice, and it was several minutes before he could loosen it. But his teeth finally pulled it apart, and with the reins in his hands he sprang upon the wheel. And as he stood so, a shock of fear ran down his back like an electric current, his breath left him, and he stood immovable, gazing with wide eyes into the darkness.

The officer with the lantern had suddenly loomed up from behind a carriage not fifty feet distant, and was standing perfectly still, with his lantern held over his head, peering so directly toward Gallegher that the boy felt that he must see him. Gallegher stood with one foot on the hub of the wheel and with the other on the box waiting to spring. It seemed a minute before either of them moved, and then the officer took a step forward, and demanded sternly, "Who is that? What are you doing there?"

There was no time for parley then. Gallegher felt that he had been taken in the act, and that his only chance lay in open flight. He leaped up on the box, pulling out the whip as he did so, and with a quick sweep lashed the horse across the head and back. The animal sprang forward with a snort, narrowly clearing the gate-post, and plunged off into the darkness.

"Stop!" cried the officer.

So many of Gallegher's acquaintances among the 'longshoremen and mill hands had been challenged in so much the same manner that Gallegher knew what would probably follow if the challenge was disregarded. So he slipped from his seat to the footboard below, and ducked his head.

The three reports of a pistol, which rang out briskly from behind him, proved that his early training had given him a valuable fund of useful miscellaneous knowledge.

"Don't you be scared," he said, reassuringly, to the horse; "he's firing in the air."

The pistol-shots were answered by the impatient clangor of a patrol-wagon's gong, and glancing over his shoulder Gallegher saw its red and green lanterns tossing from side to side and looking in the darkness like the side-lights of a yacht plunging forward in a storm.

"I hadn't bargained to race you against no patrol-wagons," said Gallegher to his animal; "but if they want a race, we'll give them a tough tussle for it, won't we?"

Philadelphia, lying four miles to the south, sent up a faint yellow glow to the sky. It seemed very far away, and Gallegher's braggadocio grew cold within him at the loneliness of his adventure and the thought of the long ride before him.

It was still bitterly cold.

The rain and sleet beat through his clothes, and struck his skin with a sharp, chilling touch that set him trembling.

Even the thought of the over-weighted patrol-wagon probably sticking in the mud some safe distance in the rear, failed to cheer him, and the excitement that had so far made him callous to the cold died out and left him weaker and nervous.

But his horse was chilled with the long standing, and now leaped eagerly forward, only too willing to warm the half-frozen blood in its veins.

"You're a good beast," said Gallegher, plaintively. "You've got more nerve than me. Don't you go back on me now. Mr. Dwyer says we've got to beat the town." Gallegher had no idea what time it was as he rode through the night, but he knew he would be able to find out from a big clock over a manufactory at a point nearly three-quarters of the distance from Keppler's to the goal.

He was still in the open country and driving recklessly, for he knew the best part of his ride must be made outside the city limits.

He raced between desolate-looking cornfields with bare stalks and patches of muddy earth rising above the thin covering of snow; truck farms and brick-yards fell behind him on either side. It was very lonely work, and once or twice the dogs ran yelping to the gates and barked after him.

Part of his way lay parallel with the railroad tracks, and he drove for some time beside long lines of freight and coal cars as they stood resting for the night. The fantastic Queen Anne suburban stations were dark and deserted, but in one or two of the block-towers he could see the operators writing at their desks, and the sight in some way comforted him.

Once he thought of stopping to get out the blanket in which he had wrapped himself on the first trip, but he feared to spare the time, and drove on with his teeth chattering and his shoulders shaking with the cold.

He welcomed the first solitary row of darkened houses with a faint cheer of recognition. The scattered lamp-posts lightened his spirits, and even the badly paved streets rang under the beats of his horse's feet like music. Great mills and manufactories, with only a night-watchman's light in the lowest of their many stories, began to take the place of the gloomy farm-houses and gaunt trees that had startled him with their grotesque shapes. He had been driving nearly an hour, he calculated, and in that time the rain had changed to a wet snow, that fell heavily and clung to whatever it touched. He passed block after block of trim work-men's houses, as still and silent as the sleepers within them, and at last he turned the horse's head into Broad Street, the city's great thoroughfare, that stretches from its one end to the other and cuts it evenly in two.

He was driving noiselessly over the snow and slush in the street, with his thoughts bent only on the clock-face he wished so much to see, when a hoarse voice challenged him from the sidewalk. "Hey, you, stop there, hold up!" said the voice.

Gallegher turned his head, and though he saw that the voice came from under a policeman's helmet, his only answer was to hit his horse sharply over the head with his whip and to urge it into a gallop.

This, on his part, was followed by a sharp, shrill whistle from the policeman. Another whistle answered it from a street-corner one block ahead of him. "Whoa," said Gallegher, pulling on the reins. "There's one too many of them," he added, in apologetic explanation. The horse stopped, and stood, breathing heavily, with great clouds of steam rising from its flanks.

"Why in hell didn't you stop when I told you to?" demanded the voice, now close at the cab's side.

"I didn't hear you," returned Gallegher, sweetly. "But I heard you whistle, and I heard your partner whistle, and I thought maybe it was me you wanted to speak to, so I just stopped."

"You heard me well enough. Why aren't your lights lit?" demanded the voice.

"Should I have 'em lit?" asked Gallegher, bending over and regarding them with sudden interest.

"You know you should, and if you don't, you've no right to be driving that cab. I don't believe you're the regular driver, anyway. Where'd you get it?"

"It ain't my cab, of course," said Gallegher, with an easy laugh. "It's Luke McGovern's. He left it outside Cronin's while he went in to get a drink, and he took too much, and me father told me to drive it round to the stable for him. I'm Cronin's son. McGovern ain't in no condition to drive. You can see yourself how he's been misusing the horse. He puts it up at Bachman's livery stable, and I was just going around there now."

Gallegher's knowledge of the local celebrities of the district confused the zealous officer of the peace. He surveyed the boy with a steady stare that would have distressed a less skilful liar, but Gallegher only shrugged his shoulders slightly, as if from the cold, and waited with apparent indifference to what the officer would say next.

In reality his heart was beating heavily against his side, and he felt that if he was kept on a strain much longer he would give way and break down. A second snow-covered form emerged suddenly from the shadow of the houses.

"What is it, Reeder?" it asked.

"Oh, nothing much," replied the first officer. "This kid hadn't any lamps lit, so I called to him to stop and he didn't do it, so I whistled to you. It's all right, though. He's just taking it round to Bachman's. Go ahead," he added, sulkily.

"Get up!" chirped Gallegher. "Good night," he added, over his shoulder.

Gallegher gave a hysterical little gasp of relief as he trotted away from the two policemen, and poured bitter maledictions on their heads for two meddling fools as he went.

"They might as well kill a man as scare him to death," he said, with an attempt to get back to his customary flippancy. But the effort was somewhat pitiful, and he felt guiltily conscious that a salt, warm tear was creeping slowly down his face, and that a lump that would not keep down was rising in his throat.

"Tain't no fair thing for the whole police force to keep worrying at a little boy like me," he said, in shame-faced apology. "I'm not doing nothing wrong, and I'm half froze to death, and yet they keep a-nagging at me."

It was so cold that when the boy stamped his feet against the footboard to keep them warm, sharp pains shot up through his body, and when he beat his arms about his shoulders, as he had seen real cabmen do, the blood in his finger-tips tingled so acutely that he cried aloud with the pain.

He had often been up that late before, but he had never felt so sleepy. It was as if some one was pressing a sponge heavy with chloroform near his face, and he could not fight off the drowsiness that lay hold of him.

He saw, dimly hanging above his head, a round disk of light that seemed like a great moon, and which he finally guessed to be the clock-face for which he had been on the lookout. He had passed it before he realized this; but the fact stirred him into wakefulness again, and when his cab's wheels slipped around the City Hall corner, he remembered to look up at the other big clock-face that keeps awake over the railroad station and measures out the night.

He gave a gasp of consternation when he saw that it was half-past two, and that there was but ten minutes left to him. This, and the many electric lights and the sight of the familiar pile of buildings, startled him into a semi-consciousness of where he was and how great was the necessity for haste.

He rose in his seat and called on the horse, and urged it into a reckless gallop over the slippery asphalt. He considered nothing else but speed, and looking neither to the left nor right dashed off down Broad Street into Chestnut, where his course lay straight away to the office, now only seven blocks distant.

Gallegher never knew how it began, but he was suddenly assaulted by shouts on either side, his horse was thrown back on its haunches, and he found two men in cabmen's livery hanging at its head, and patting its sides, and calling it by name. And the other cabmen who have their stand at the corner were swarming about the carriage, all of them talking and swearing at once, and gesticulating wildly with their whips.

They said they knew the cab was McGovern's, and they wanted to know where he was, and why he wasn't on it; they wanted to know where Gallegher had stolen it, and why he had been such a fool as to drive it into the arms of its owner's friends; they said that it was about time that a cab-driver could get off his box to take a drink without having his cab run away with, and some of them called loudly for a policeman to take the young thief in charge.

Gallagher felt as if he had been suddenly dragged into consciousness out of a bad dream, and stood for a second like a half-awakened somnambulist.

They had stopped the cab under an electric light, and its glare shone coldly down upon the trampled snow and the faces of the men around him.

Gallegher bent forward, and lashed savagely at the horse with his whip.

"Let me go," he shouted, as he tugged impotently at the reins. "Let me go, I tell you. I haven't stole no cab, and you've got no right to stop me. I only want to take it to the Press office," he begged. "They'll send it back to you all right. They'll pay you for the trip. I'm not running away with it. The driver's got the collar—he's 'rested—and I'm only a-going to the Press office. Do you hear me?" he cried, his voice rising and breaking in a shriek of passion and disappointment. "I tell you to let go those reins. Let me go, or I'll kill you. Do you hear me? I'll kill you." And leaning forward, the boy struck savagely with his long whip at the faces of the men about the horse's head.

Some one in the crowd reached up and caught him by the ankles, and with a quick jerk pulled him off the box, and threw him on to the street. But he was up on his knees in a moment, and caught at the man's hand.

"Don't let them stop me, mister," he cried, "please let me go. I didn't steal the cab, sir. S'help me, I didn't. I'm telling you the truth. Take me to the Press office, and they'll prove it to you. They'll pay you anything you ask 'em. It's only such a little ways now, and I've come so far, sir. Please don't let them stop me," he sobbed, clasping the man about the knees. "For Heaven's sake, mister, let me go!"

The managing editor of the Press took up the india-rubber speaking-tube at his side, and answered, "Not yet," to an inquiry the night editor had already put to him five times within the last twenty minutes.

Then he snapped the metal top of the tube impatiently, and went up-stairs. As he passed the door of the local room, he noticed that the reporters had not gone home, but were sitting about on the tables and chairs, waiting. They looked up inquiringly as he passed, and the city editor asked, "Any news yet?" and the managing editor shook his head.

The compositors were standing idle in the composing-room, and their foreman was talking with the night editor.

"Well," said that gentleman, tentatively.

"Well," returned the managing editor, "I don't think we can wait; do you?"

"It's a half-hour after time now," said the night editor, "and we'll miss the suburban trains if we hold the paper back any longer. We can't afford to wait for a purely hypothetical story. The chances are all against the fight's having taken place or this Hade's having been arrested."

"But if we're beaten on it–" suggested the chief. "But I don't think that is possible. If there were any story to print, Dwyer would have had it here before now."

The managing editor looked steadily down at the floor.

"Very well," he said, slowly, "we won't wait any longer. Go ahead," he added, turning to the foreman with a sigh of reluctance. The foreman whirled himself about, and began to give his orders; but the two editors still looked at each other doubtfully.

As they stood so, there came a sudden shout and the sound of people running to and fro in the reportorial rooms below. There was the tramp of many footsteps on the stairs, and above the confusion they heard the voice of the city editor telling some one to "run to Madden's and get some brandy, quick."

No one in the composing-room said anything; but those compositors who had started to go home began slipping off their overcoats, and every one stood with his eyes fixed on the door.

It was kicked open from the outside, and in the doorway stood a cab-driver and the city editor, supporting between them a pitiful little figure of a boy, wet and miserable, and with the snow melting on his clothes and running in little pools to the floor. "Why, it's Gallegher," said the night editor, in a tone of the keenest disappointment.

Gallegher shook himself free from his supporters, and took an unsteady step forward, his fingers fumbling stiffly with the buttons of his waistcoat.

"Mr. Dwyer, sir," he began faintly, with his eyes fixed fearfully on the managing editor, "he got arrested—and I couldn't get here no sooner, 'cause they kept a-stopping me, and they took me cab from under me—but—" he pulled the notebook from his breast and held it out with its covers damp and limp from the rain—"but we got Hade, and here's Mr. Dwyer's copy."

And then he asked, with a queer note in his voice, partly of dread and partly of hope, "Am I in time, sir?"

The managing editor took the book, and tossed it to the foreman, who ripped out its leaves and dealt them out to his men as rapidly as a gambler deals out cards.

Then the managing editor stooped and picked Gallegher up in his arms, and, sitting down, began to unlace his wet and muddy shoes.

Gallegher made a faint effort to resist this degradation of the managerial dignity; but his protest was a very feeble one, and his head fell back heavily oh the managing editor's shoulder.

To Gallegher the incandescent lights began to whirl about in circles, and to burn in different colors; the faces of the reporters kneeling before him and chafing his hands and feet grew dim and unfamiliar, and the roar and rumble of the great presses in the basement sounded far away, like the murmur of the sea.

"Why, it's Gallegher," said the night editor.

And then the place and the circumstances of it came back to him again sharply and with sudden vividness.

Gallegher looked up, with a faint smile, into the managing editor's face. "You won't turn me off for running away, will you?" he whispered.

The managing editor did not answer immediately. His head was bent, and he was thinking, for some reason or other, of a little boy of his own, at home in bed. Then he said quietly, "Not this time, Gallegher."

Gallegher's head sank back comfortably on the older man's shoulder, and he smiled comprehensively at the faces of the young men crowded around him. "You hadn't ought to," he said, with a touch of his old impudence, '"cause–I beat the town."

BLOOD WILL TELL

David Greene was an employee of the Burdett Automatic Punch Company. The manufacturing plant of the company was at Bridgeport, but in the New York offices there were working samples of all the punches, from the little nickel-plated hand punch with which conductors squeezed holes in railroad tickets, to the big punch that could bite into an iron plate as easily as into a piece of pie. David's duty was to explain these different punches, and accordingly when Burdett Senior or one of the sons turned a customer over to David he spoke of him as a salesman. But David called himself a "demonstrator." For a short time he even succeeded in persuading the other salesmen to speak of themselves as demonstrators, but the shipping clerks and bookkeepers laughed them out of it. They could not laugh David out of it. This was so, partly because he had no sense of humor, and partly because he had a great-great-grandfather. Among the salesmen on lower Broadway, to possess a great-great-grandfather is unusual, even a great-grandfather is a rarity, and either is considered superfluous. But to David the possession of a great-great-grandfather was a precious and open delight. He had possessed him only for a short time. Undoubtedly he always had existed, but it was not until David's sister Anne married a doctor in Bordentown, New Jersey, and became socially ambitious, that David emerged as a Son of Washington.

It was sister Anne, anxious to "get in" as a "Daughter" and wear a distaff pin in her shirt-waist, who discovered the revolutionary ancestor. She unearthed him, or rather ran him to earth, in the graveyard of the Presbyterian church at Bordentown. He was no less a person than General Hiram Greene, and he had fought with Washington at Trenton and at Princeton. Of this there was no doubt. That, later, on moving to New York, his descendants became peace-loving salesmen did not affect his record. To enter a society founded on heredity, the important thing is first to catch your ancestor, and having made sure of him, David entered the Society of the Sons of Washington with flying colors. He was not unlike the man who had been speaking prose for forty years without knowing it. He was not unlike the other man who woke to find himself famous. He had gone to bed a timid, near-sighted, underpaid salesman without a relative in the world, except a married sister in Bordentown, and he awoke to find he was a direct descendant of "Neck or Nothing" Greene, a revolutionary hero, a friend of Washington, a man whose portrait hung in the State House at Trenton. David's life had lacked color. The day he carried his certificate of membership to the big jewelry store uptown and purchased two rosettes, one for each of his two coats, was the proudest of his life.

The other men in the Broadway office took a different view. As Wyckoff, one of Burdett's flying squadron of travelling salesmen, said, "All grandfathers look alike to me, whether they're great, or great-great-great. Each one is as dead as the other. I'd rather have a live cousin who could loan me a five, or slip me a drink. What did your great-great dad ever do for you?"

"Well, for one thing," said David stiffly, "he fought in the War of the Revolution. He saved us from the shackles of monarchical England; he made it possible for me and you to enjoy the liberties of a free republic."

"Don't try to tell me your grandfather did all that," protested Wyckoff, "because I know better. There were a lot of others helped. I read about it in a book."

"I am not grudging glory to others," returned David; "I am only saying I am proud that I am a descendant of a revolutionist."

Wyckoff dived into his inner pocket and produced a leather photograph frame that folded like a concertina.

"I don't want to be a descendant," he said; "I'd rather be an ancestor. Look at those." Proudly he exhibited photographs of Mrs. Wyckoff with the baby and of three other little Wyckoffs. David looked with envy at the children.

"When I'm married," he stammered, and at the words he blushed, "I hope to be an ancestor."

"If you're thinking of getting married," said Wyckoff, "you'd better hope for a raise in salary."

The other clerks were as unsympathetic as Wyckoff. At first when David showed them his parchment certificate, and his silver gilt insignia with on one side a portrait of Washington, and on the other a Continental soldier, they admitted it was dead swell. They even envied him, not the grandfather, but the fact that owing to that distinguished relative David was constantly receiving beautifully engraved invitations to attend the monthly meetings of the society; to subscribe to a fund to erect monuments on battle-fields to mark neglected graves; to join in joyous excursions to the tomb of Washington or of John Paul

Jones; to inspect West Point, Annapolis, and Bunker Hill; to be among those present at the annual "banquet" at Delmonico's. In order that when he opened these letters he might have an audience, he had given the society his office address.

In these communications he was always addressed as "Dear Compatriot," and never did the words fail to give him a thrill. They seemed to lift him out of Burdett's salesrooms and Broadway, and place him next to things uncommercial, untainted, high, and noble. He did not quite know what an aristocrat was, but he believed being a compatriot made him an aristocrat. When customers were rude, when Mr. John or Mr. Robert was overbearing, this idea enabled David to rise above their ill-temper, and he would smile and say to himself: "If they knew the meaning of the blue rosette in my button-hole, how differently they would treat me! How easily with a word could I crush them!"

But few of the customers recognized the significance of the button. They thought it meant that David belonged to the Y. M. C. A. or was a teetotaler. David, with his gentle manners and pale, ascetic face, was liable to give that impression.

When Wyckoff mentioned marriage, the reason David blushed was because, although no one in the office suspected it, he wished to marry the person in whom the office took the greatest pride. This was Miss Emily Anthony, one of Burdett and Sons' youngest, most efficient, and prettiest stenographers, and although David did not cut as dashing a figure as did some of the firm's travelling men, Miss Anthony had found something in him so greatly to admire that she had, out of office hours, accepted his devotion, his theatre tickets, and an engagement ring. Indeed, so far had matters progressed, that it had been almost decided when in a few months they would go upon their vacations they also would go upon their honeymoon. And then a cloud had come between them, and from a quarter from which David had expected only sunshine.

The trouble befell when David discovered he had a great-great-grandfather. With that fact itself Miss Anthony was almost as pleased as was David himself, but while he was content to bask in another's glory, Miss Anthony saw in his inheritance only an incentive to achieve glory for himself.

From a hard-working salesman she had asked but little, but from a descendant of a national hero she expected other things. She was a determined young person, and for David she was an ambitious young person. She found she was dissatisfied. She found she was disappointed. The great-great-grandfather had opened up a new horizon–had, in a way, raised the standard. She was as fond of David as always, but his tales of past wars and battles, his accounts of present banquets at which he sat shoulder to shoulder with men of whom even Burdett and Sons spoke with awe, touched her imagination.

"You shouldn't be content to just wear a button," she urged. "If you're a Son of Washington, you ought to act like one."

"I know I'm not worthy of you," David sighed.

"I don't mean that, and you know I don't," Emily replied indignantly. "It has nothing to do with me! I want you to be worthy of yourself, of your grandpa Hiram!"

"But how?" complained David. "What chance has a twenty-five dollar a week clerk—"

It was a year before the Spanish-American War, while the patriots of Cuba were fighting the mother country for their independence.

"If I were a Son of the Revolution," said Emily, "I'd go to Cuba and help free it."

"Don't talk nonsense," cried David. "If I did that I'd lose my job, and we'd never be able to marry. Besides, what's Cuba done for me? All I know about Cuba is, I once smoked a Cuban cigar and it made me ill."

"Did Lafayette talk like that?" demanded Emily. "Did he ask what have the American rebels ever done for me?"

"If I were in Lafayette's class," sighed David, "I wouldn't be selling automatic punches."

"There's your trouble," declared Emily. "You lack self-confidence. You're too humble, you've got fighting blood and you ought to keep saying to yourself, 'Blood will tell,' and the first thing you know, it will tell! You might begin by going into politics in your ward. Or, you could join the militia. That takes only one night a week, and then, if we did go to war with Spain, you'd get a commission, and come back a captain!"

Emily's eyes were beautiful with delight. But the sight gave David no pleasure. In genuine distress, he shook his head.

"Emily," he said, "you're going to be awfully disappointed in me."

Emily's eyes closed as though they shied at some mental picture. But when she opened them they were bright, and her smile was kind and eager.

"No, I'm not," she protested; "only I want a husband with a career, and one who'll tell me to keep quiet when I try to run it for him."

"I've often wished you would," said David.

"Would what? Run your career for you?"

"No, keep quiet. Only it didn't seem polite to tell you so."

"Maybe I'd like you better," said Emily, "if you weren't so darned polite."

A week later, early in the spring of 1897, the unexpected happened, and David was promoted into the flying squadron. He now was a travelling salesman, with a rise in salary and a commission on orders. It was a step forward, but as going on the road meant absence from Emily, David was not elated. Nor did it satisfy Emily. It was not money she wanted. Her ambition for David could not be silenced with a raise in wages. She did not say this, but David knew that in him she still found something lacking, and when they said good-by they both were ill at ease and completely unhappy. Formerly, each day when Emily in passing David in the office said good-morning, she used to add the number of the days that still separated them from the vacation which also was to be their honeymoon. But, for the last month she had stopped counting the days–at least she did not count them aloud.

David did not ask her why this was so. He did not dare. And, sooner than learn the truth that she had decided not to marry him, or that she was even considering not marrying him, he asked no questions, but in ignorance of her present feelings set forth on his travels. Absence from Emily hurt just as much as he had feared it would. He missed her, needed her, longed for her. In numerous letters he told her so. But, owing to the frequency with which he moved, her letters never caught up with him. It was almost a relief. He did not care to think of what they might tell him.

The route assigned David took him through the South and kept him close to the Atlantic seaboard. In obtaining orders he was not unsuccessful, and at the end of the first month received from the firm a telegram of congratulation. This was of importance chiefly because it might please Emily. But he knew that in her eyes the great-great-grandson of Hiram Greene could not rest content with a telegram from Burdett and Sons. A year before she would have considered it a high honor, a cause for celebration. Now, he could see her press her pretty lips together and shake her pretty head. It was not enough. But how could he accomplish more. He began to hate his great-great-grandfather. He began to wish Hiram Greene had lived and died a bachelor.

And then Dame Fortune took David in hand and toyed with him and spanked him, and pelted and petted him, until finally she made him her favorite son. Dame Fortune went about this work in an abrupt and arbitrary manner.

On the night of the 1st of March, 1897, two trains were scheduled to leave the Union Station at Jacksonville at exactly the same minute, and they left exactly on time. As never before in the history of any Southern railroad has this miracle occurred, it shows that when Dame Fortune gets on the job she is omnipotent. She placed David on the train to Miami as the train he wanted drew out for Tampa, and an hour later, when the conductor looked at David's ticket, he pulled the bell-cord and dumped David over the side into the heart of a pine forest. If he walked back along the track for one mile, the conductor reassured him, he would find a flag station where at midnight he could flag a train going north. In an hour it would deliver him safely in Jacksonville.

There was a moon, but for the greater part of the time it was hidden by fitful, hurrying clouds, and, as David stumbled forward, at one moment he would see the rails like streaks of silver, and the next would be encompassed in a complete and bewildering darkness. He made his way from tie to tie only by feeling with his foot. After an hour he came to a shed. Whether it was or was not the flag station the conductor had in mind, he did not know, and he never did know. He was too tired, too hot, and too disgusted to proceed, and dropping his suit case he sat down under the open roof of the shed prepared to wait either for the train or daylight. So far as he could see, on every side of him stretched a swamp, silent, dismal, interminable. From its black water rose dead trees, naked of bark and hung with streamers of funereal moss. There was not a sound or sign of human habitation. The silence was the silence of the ocean at night. David remembered the berth reserved for him on the train to Tampa and of the loathing with which he had considered placing himself between its sheets. But now how gladly would he welcome it! For, in the sleeping-car, ill-smelling, close and stuffy, he at least would have been surrounded by fellow-sufferers of his own species. Here his companions were owls, water-snakes, and sleeping buzzards.

"I am alone," he told himself, "on a railroad embankment, entirely surrounded by alligators."

And then he found he was not alone.

In the darkness, illuminated by a match, not a hundred yards from him there flashed suddenly the face of a man. Then the match went out and the face with it. David noted that it had appeared at some height above the level of the swamp, at an elevation higher even than that of the embankment. It was as though the man had been sitting on the limb of a tree. David crossed the tracks and found that on the side of the embankment opposite the shed there was solid ground and what once had been a wharf. He advanced over this cautiously, and as he did so the clouds disappeared, and in the full light of the moon he saw a bayou broadening into a river, and made fast to the decayed and rotting wharf an ocean-going tug. It was from her deck that the man, in lighting his pipe, had shown his face. At the thought of a warm engine-room and the company of his fellow-creatures, David's heart leaped with pleasure. He advanced quickly. And then something in the appearance of the tug, something mysterious, secretive, threatening, caused him to halt. No lights showed from her engine-room, cabin, or pilot-house. Her decks were empty. But, as was evidenced by the black smoke that rose from her funnel, she was awake and awake to some purpose. David stood uncertainly, questioning whether to make his presence known or return to the loneliness of the shed. The question was decided for him. He had not considered that standing in the moonlight he was a conspicuous figure. The planks of the wharf creaked and a man came toward him. As one who means to attack, or who fears attack, he approached warily. He wore high boots, riding breeches, and a sombrero. He was a little man, but his movements were alert and active. To David he seemed unnecessarily excited. He thrust himself close against David.

"Who the devil are you?" demanded the man from the tug. "How'd you get here?"

"I walked," said David.

"Walked?" the man snorted incredulously.

"I took the wrong train," explained David pleasantly. "They put me off about a mile below here. I walked back to this flag station. I'm going to wait here for the next train north."

The little man laughed mockingly.

"Oh, no you're not," he said. "If you walked here, you can just walk away again!" With a sweep of his arm, he made a vigorous and peremptory gesture.

"You walk!" he commanded.

"I'll do just as I please about that," said David.

As though to bring assistance, the little man started hastily toward the tug.

"I'll find some one who'll make you walk!" he called. "You wait, that's all, you wait!"

David decided not to wait. It was possible the wharf was private property and he had been trespassing. In any case, at the flag station the rights of all men were equal, and if he were in for a fight he judged it best to choose his own battleground. He recrossed the tracks and sat down on his suit case in a dark corner of the shed. Himself hidden in the shadows he could see in the moonlight the approach of any other person.

"They're river pirates," said David to himself, "or smugglers. They're certainly up to some mischief, or why should they object to the presence of a perfectly harmless stranger?"

Partly with cold, partly with nervousness, David shivered.

"I wish that train would come," he sighed. And instantly, as though in answer to his wish, from only a short distance down the track he heard the rumble and creak of approaching cars. In a flash David planned his course of action.

The thought of spending the night in a swamp infested by alligators and smugglers had become intolerable. He must escape, and he must escape by the train now approaching. To that end the train must be stopped. His plan was simple. The train was moving very, very slowly, and though he had no lantern to wave, in order to bring it to a halt he need only stand on the track exposed to the glare of the headlight and wave his arms. David sprang between the rails and gesticulated wildly. But in amazement his arms fell to his sides. For the train, now only a hundred yards distant and creeping toward him at a snail's pace, carried no headlight, and though in the moonlight David was plainly visible, it blew no whistle, tolled no bell. Even the passenger coaches in the rear of the sightless engine were wrapped in darkness. It was a ghost of a train, a Flying Dutchman of a train, a nightmare of a train. It was as unreal as the black swamp, as the moss on the dead trees, as the ghostly tug-boat tied to the rotting wharf.

"Is the place haunted!" exclaimed David.

He was answered by the grinding of brakes and by the train coming to a sharp halt. And instantly from every side men fell from it to the ground, and the silence of the night was broken by a confusion of calls and eager greeting and questions and sharp words of command.

So fascinated was David in the stealthy arrival of the train and in her mysterious passengers that, until they confronted him, he did not note the equally stealthy approach of three men. Of these one was the little man from the tug. With him was a fat, red-faced Irish-American. He wore no coat and his shirt-sleeves were drawn away from his hands by garters of pink elastic, his derby hat was balanced behind his ears, upon his right hand flashed an enormous diamond. He looked as though but at that moment he had stopped sliding glasses across a Bowery bar. The third man carried the outward marks of a sailor. David believed he was the tallest man he had ever beheld, but equally remarkable with his height was his beard and hair, which were of a fierce brick-dust red. Even in the mild moonlight it flamed like a torch.

"What's your business?" demanded the man with the flamboyant hair.

"I came here," began David, "to wait for a train——"

The tall man bellowed with indignant rage.

"Yes," he shouted; "this is the sort of place any one would pick out to wait for a train!"

In front of David's nose he shook a fist as large as a catcher's glove. "Don't you lie to me!" he bullied. "Do you know who I am? Do you know who you're up against? I'm——"

The barkeeper person interrupted.

"Never mind who you are," he said. "We know that. Find out who he is."

David turned appealingly to the barkeeper.

"Do you suppose I'd come here on purpose?" he protested. "I'm a travelling man——"

"You won't travel any to-night," mocked the red-haired one. "You've seen what you came to see, and all you want now is to get to a Western Union wire. Well, you don't do it. You don't leave here to-night!"

As though he thought he had been neglected, the little man in riding-boots pushed forward importantly.

"Tie him to a tree!" he suggested.

"Better take him on board," said the barkeeper, "and send him back by the pilot. When we're once at sea, he can't hurt us any."

"What makes you think I want to hurt you?" demanded David. "Who do you think I am?"

In front of David's nose he shook a fist as large as a catcher's glove.

"We know who you are," shouted the fiery-headed one. "You're a blanketty-blank spy! You're a government spy or a Spanish spy, and whichever you are you don't get away to-night!"

David had not the faintest idea what the man meant, but he knew his self-respect was being ill-treated, and his self-respect rebelled.

"You have made a very serious mistake," he said, "and whether you like it or not, I am leaving here to-night, and you can go to the devil!"

Turning his back David started with great dignity to walk away. It was a short walk. Something hit him below the ear and he found himself curling up comfortably on the ties. He had a strong desire to sleep, but was conscious that a bed on a railroad track, on account of trains wanting to pass, was unsafe. This doubt did not long disturb him. His head rolled against the steel rail, his limbs relaxed. From a great distance, and in a strange sing-song he heard the voice of the barkeeper saying, "Nine—ten—and out!"

When David came to his senses his head was resting on a coil of rope. In his ears was the steady throb of an engine, and in his eyes the glare of a lantern. The lantern was held by a pleasant-faced youth in a golf cap who was smiling sympathetically. David rose on his elbow and gazed wildly about him. He was in the bow of the ocean-going tug, and he saw that from where he lay in the bow to her stern her decks were packed with men. She was steaming swiftly down a broad river. On either side the gray light that comes before the dawn showed low banks studded with stunted palmettos. Close ahead David heard the roar of the surf.

"Sorry to disturb you," said the youth in the golf cap, "but we drop the pilot in a few minutes and you're going with him."

David moved his aching head gingerly, and was conscious of a bump as large as a tennis ball behind his right ear.

"What happened to me?" he demanded.

"You were sort of kidnapped, I guess," laughed the young man. "It was a raw deal, but they couldn't take any chances. The pilot will land you at Okra Point. You can hire a rig there to take you to the railroad."

"But why?" demanded David indignantly. "Why was I kidnapped? What had I done? Who were those men who—"

From the pilot-house there was a sharp jangle of bells to the engine-room, and the speed of the tug slackened.

"Come on," commanded the young man briskly. "The pilot's going ashore. Here's your grip, here's your hat. The ladder's on the port side. Look where you're stepping. We can't show any lights, and it's dark as—"

But, even as he spoke, like a flash of powder, as swiftly as one throws an electric switch, as blindingly as a train leaps from the tunnel into the glaring sun, the darkness vanished and the tug was swept by the fierce, blatant radiance of a search-light.

It was met by shrieks from two hundred throats, by screams, oaths, prayers, by the sharp jangling of bells, by the blind rush of many men scurrying like rats for a hole to hide in, by the ringing orders of one man. Above the tumult this one voice rose like the warning strokes of a fire-gong, and looking up to the pilot-house from whence the voice came, David saw the barkeeper still in his shirt-sleeves and with his derby hat pushed back behind his ears, with one hand clutching the telegraph to the engine-room, with the other holding the spoke of the wheel.

David felt the tug, like a hunter taking a fence, rise in a great leap. Her bow sank and rose, tossing the water from her in black, oily waves, the smoke poured from her funnel, from below her engines sobbed and quivered, and like a hound freed from a leash she raced for the open sea. But swiftly as she fled, as a thief is held in the circle of a policeman's bull's-eye, the shaft of light followed and exposed her and held her in its grip. The youth in the golf cap was clutching David by the arm. With his free hand he pointed down the shaft of light. So great was the tumult that to be heard he brought his lips close to David's ear.

"That's the revenue cutter!" he shouted. "She's been laying for us for three weeks, and now," he shrieked exultingly, "the old man's going to give her a race for it."

From excitement, from cold, from alarm, David's nerves were getting beyond his control.

"But how," he demanded, "how do I get ashore?"

"You don't!"

"When he drops the pilot, don't I—"

"How can he drop the pilot?" yelled the youth. "The pilot's got to stick by the boat. So have you."

David clutched the young man and swung him so that they stood face to face.

"Stick by what boat?" yelled David. "Who are these men? Who are you? What boat is this?"

In the glare of the search-light David saw the eyes of the youth staring at him as though he feared he were in the clutch of a madman. Wrenching himself free, the youth pointed at the pilot-house. Above it on a blue board in letters of gold-leaf a foot high was the name of the tug. As David read it his breath left him, a finger of ice passed slowly down his spine. The name he read was The Three Friends.

"The Three Friends!" shrieked David. "She's a filibuster! She's a pirate! Where're we going?"

"To Cuba!"

David emitted a howl of anguish, rage, and protest.

"What for?" he shrieked.

The young man regarded him coldly.

"To pick bananas," he said.

"I won't go to Cuba," shouted David. "I've got to work! I'm paid to sell machinery. I demand to be put ashore. I'll lose my job if I'm not put ashore. I'll sue you! I'll have the law—"

David found himself suddenly upon his knees. His first thought was that the ship had struck a rock, and then that she was bumping herself over a succession of coral reefs. She dipped, dived, reared, and plunged. Like a hooked fish, she flung herself in the air, quivering from bow to stern. No longer was David of a mind to sue the filibusters if they did not put him ashore. If only they had put him ashore, in gratitude he would have crawled on his knees. What followed was of no interest to David, nor to many of the filibusters, nor to any of the Cuban patriots. Their groans of self-pity, their prayers and curses in eloquent Spanish, rose high above the crash of broken crockery and the pounding of the waves. Even when the search-light gave way to a brilliant sunlight the circumstance was unobserved by David. Nor was he concerned in the tidings brought forward by the youth in the golf cap, who raced the slippery decks and vaulted the prostrate forms as sure-footedly as a hurdler on a cinder track. To David, in whom he seemed to think he had found a congenial spirit, he shouted joyfully, "She's fired two blanks at us!" he cried; "now she's firing cannon-balls!"

"Thank God," whispered David; "perhaps she'll sink us!"

But The Three Friends showed her heels to the revenue cutter, and so far as David knew hours passed into days and days into weeks. It was like those nightmares in which in a minute one is whirled through centuries of fear and torment. Sometimes, regardless of nausea, of his aching head, of the hard deck, of the waves that splashed and smothered him, David fell into broken slumber. Sometimes he woke to a dull consciousness of his position. At such moments he added to his misery by speculating upon the other misfortunes that might have befallen him on shore. Emily, he decided, had given him up for lost and married–probably a navy officer in command of a battle-ship. Burdett and Sons had cast him off forever. Possibly his disappearance had caused them to suspect him; even now they might be regarding him as a defaulter, as a fugitive from justice. His accounts, no doubt, were being carefully overhauled. In actual time, two days and two nights had passed; to David it seemed many ages.

On the third day he crawled to the stern, where there seemed less motion, and finding a boat's cushion threw it in the lee scupper and fell upon it. From time to time the youth in the golf cap had brought him food and drink, and he now appeared from the cook's galley bearing a bowl of smoking soup.

David considered it a doubtful attention.

But he said, "You're very kind. How did a fellow like you come to mix up with these pirates?"

The youth laughed good-naturedly.

"They're not pirates, they're patriots," he said, "and I'm not mixed up with them. My name is Henry Carr and I'm a guest of Jimmy Doyle, the captain."

"The barkeeper with the derby hat?" said David.

"He's not a barkeeper, he's a teetotaler," Carr corrected, "and he's the greatest filibuster alive. He knows these waters as you know Broadway, and he's the salt of the earth. I did him a favor once; sort of mouse-helping-the-lion idea. Just through dumb luck I found out about this expedition. The government agents in New York found out I'd found out and sent for me to tell. But I didn't, and I didn't write the story either. Doyle heard about that. So, he asked me to come as his guest, and he's promised that after he's landed the expedition and the arms I can write as much about it as I darn please."

"Then you're a reporter?" said David.

"I'm what we call a cub reporter," laughed Carr. "You see, I've always dreamed of being a war correspondent. The men in the office say I dream too much. They're always guying me about it. But, haven't you noticed, it's the ones who dream who find their dreams come true. Now this isn't real war, but it's a near war, and when the real thing breaks loose, I can tell the managing editor I served as a war correspondent in the Cuban-Spanish campaign. And he may give me a real job!"

"And you like this?" groaned David.

"I wouldn't, if I were as sick as you are," said Carr, "but I've a stomach like a Harlem goat." He stooped and lowered his voice. "Now, here are two fake filibusters," he whispered. "The men you read about in the newspapers. If a man's a real filibuster, nobody knows it!"

Coming toward them was the tall man who had knocked David out, and the little one who had wanted to tie him to a tree.

"All they ask," whispered Carr, "is money and advertisement. If they knew I was a reporter, they'd eat out of my hand. The tall man calls himself Lighthouse Harry. He once kept a lighthouse on the Florida coast, and that's as near to the sea as he ever got. The other one is a daredevil calling himself Colonel Beamish. He says he's an English officer, and a soldier of fortune, and that he's been in eighteen battles. Jimmy says he's never been near enough to a battle to see the red-cross flags on the base hospital. But they've fooled these Cubans. The Junta thinks they're great fighters, and it's sent them down here to work the machine guns. But I'm afraid the only fighting they will do will be in the sporting columns, and not in the ring."

A half dozen sea-sick Cubans were carrying a heavy, oblong box. They dropped it not two yards from where David lay, and with a screw-driver Lighthouse Harry proceeded to open the lid.

Carr explained to David that The Three Friends was approaching that part of the coast of Cuba on which she had arranged to land her expedition, and that in case she was surprised by one of the Spanish patrol boats she was preparing to defend herself.

"They've got an automatic gun in that crate," said Carr, "and they're going to assemble it. You'd better move; they'll be tramping all over you."

David shook his head feebly.

"I can't move!" he protested. "I wouldn't move if it would free Cuba."

For several hours with very languid interest David watched Lighthouse Harry and Colonel Beamish screw a heavy tripod to the deck and balance above it a quick-firing one-pounder. They worked very slowly, and to David, watching them from the lee scupper, they appeared extremely unintelligent.

"I don't believe either of those thugs put an automatic gun together in his life," he whispered to Carr. "I never did, either, but I've put hundreds of automatic punches together, and I bet that gun won't work."

"What's wrong with it?" said Carr.

Before David could summon sufficient energy to answer, the attention of all on board was diverted, and by a single word.

Whether the word is whispered apologetically by the smoking-room steward to those deep in bridge, or shrieked from the tops of a sinking ship it never quite fails of its effect. A sweating stoker from the engine-room saw it first.

"Land!" he hailed.

The sea-sick Cubans raised themselves and swung their hats; their voices rose in a fierce chorus.

"Cuba libre!" they yelled.

The sun piercing the morning mists had uncovered a coast-line broken with bays and inlets. Above it towered green hills, the peak of each topped by a squat block-house; in the valleys and water courses like columns of marble rose the royal palms.

"You must look!" Carr entreated David. "It's just as it is in the pictures!"

"Then I don't have to look," groaned David.

The Three Friends was making for a point of land that curved like a sickle. On the inside of the sickle was Nipe Bay. On the opposite shore of that broad harbor at the place of rendezvous a little band of Cubans waited to receive the filibusters. The goal was in sight. The dreadful voyage was done. Joy and excitement thrilled the ship's company. Cuban patriots appeared in uniforms with Cuban flags pinned in the brims of their straw sombreros. From the hold came boxes of small-arm ammunition, of Mausers, rifles, machetes, and saddles. To protect the landing a box of shells was placed in readiness beside the one-pounder.

"In two hours, if we have smooth water," shouted Lighthouse Harry, "we ought to get all of this on shore. And then, all I ask," he cried mightily, "is for some one to kindly show me a Spaniard!"

His heart's desire was instantly granted. He was shown not only one Spaniard, but several Spaniards. They were on the deck of one of the fastest gun-boats of the Spanish navy. Not a mile from The Three Friends she sprang from the cover of a narrow inlet. She did not signal questions or extend courtesies. For her the name of the ocean-going tug was sufficient introduction. Throwing ahead of her a solid shell, she raced in pursuit, and as The Three Friends leaped to full speed there came from the gun-boat the sharp dry crackle of Mausers.

With an explosion of terrifying oaths Lighthouse Harry thrust a shell into the breech of the quick-firing gun. Without waiting to aim it, he tugged at the trigger. Nothing happened! He threw open the breech and gazed impotently at the base of the shell. It was untouched. The ship was ringing with cries of anger, of hate, with rat-like squeaks of fear.

Above the heads of the filibusters a shell screamed and within a hundred feet splashed into a wave.

From his mat in the lee scupper David groaned miserably. He was far removed from any of the greater emotions.

"It's no use!" he protested. "They can't do! It's not connected!"

"What's not connected?" yelled Carr. He fell upon David. He half-lifted, half-dragged him to his feet.

"If you know what's wrong with that gun, you fix it! Fix it," he shouted, "or I'll—"

David was not concerned with the vengeance Carr threatened. For, on the instant a miracle had taken place. With the swift insidiousness of morphine, peace ran through his veins, soothed his racked body, his jangled nerves. The Three Friends had made the harbor, and was gliding through water flat as a pond. But David did not know why the change had come. He knew only that his soul and body were at rest, that the sun was shining, that he had passed through the valley of the shadow, and once more was a sane, sound young man.

With a savage thrust of the shoulder he sent Lighthouse Harry sprawling from the gun. With swift, practised fingers he fell upon its mechanism. He wrenched it apart. He lifted it, reset, readjusted it.

Ignorant themselves, those about him saw that he understood, saw that his work was good.

They raised a joyous, defiant cheer. But a shower of bullets drove them to cover, bullets that ripped the deck, splintered the superstructure, smashed the glass in the air ports, like angry wasps sang in a continuous whining chorus. Intent only on the gun, David worked feverishly. He swung to the breech, locked it, and dragged it open, pulled on the trigger and found it gave before his forefinger.

He shouted with delight.

"I've got it working," he yelled.

He turned to his audience, but his audience had fled. From beneath one of the life-boats protruded the riding-boots of Colonel Beamish, the tall form of Lighthouse Harry was doubled behind a water butt. A shell splashed to port, a shell splashed to starboard. For an instant David stood staring wide-eyed at the greyhound of a boat that ate up the distance between them, at the jets of smoke and stabs of flame that sprang from her bow, at the figures crouched behind her gunwale, firing in volleys.

To David it came suddenly, convincingly, that in a dream he had lived it all before, and something like raw poison stirred in David, something leaped to his throat and choked him, something rose in his brain and made him see scarlet. He felt rather than saw young Carr kneeling at the box of ammunition, and holding a shell toward him. He heard the click as the breech shut, felt the rubber tire of the brace give against the weight of his shoulder, down a long shining tube saw the pursuing gun-boat, saw her again and many times disappear behind a flash of flame. A bullet gashed his forehead, a bullet passed deftly through his forearm, but he did not heed them. Confused with the thrashing of the engines, with the roar of the gun he heard a strange voice shrieking unceasingly:

"Cuba libre!" it yelled. "To hell with Spain!" and he found that the voice was his own.

The story lost nothing in the way Carr wrote it.

"And the best of it is," he exclaimed joyfully, "it's true!"

For a Spanish gun-boat had been crippled and forced to run herself aground by a tug-boat manned by Cuban patriots, and by a single gun served by one man, and that man an American. It was the first sea-fight of the war. Over night a Cuban navy had been born, and into the limelight a cub reporter had projected a new "hero," a ready-made, warranted-not-to-run, popular idol.

They were seated in the pilot-house, "Jimmy" Doyle, Carr, and David, the patriots and their arms had been safely dumped upon the coast of Cuba, and The Three Friends was gliding swiftly and, having caught the Florida straits napping, smoothly toward Key West. Carr had just finished reading aloud his account of the engagement.

"You will tell the story just as I have written it," commanded the proud author.

"Your being South as a travelling salesman was only a blind. You came to volunteer for this expedition. Before you could explain your wish you were mistaken for a secret-service man, and hustled on board. That was just where you wanted to be, and when the moment arrived you took command of the ship and single-handed won the naval battle of Nipe Bay."

Jimmy Doyle nodded his head approvingly. "You certainly did, Dave," protested the great man, "I seen you when you done it!"

At Key West Carr filed his story and while the hospital surgeons kept David there over one steamer, to dress his wounds, his fame and features spread across the map of the United States.

Burdett and Sons basked in reflected glory. Reporters besieged their office. At the Merchants Down-Town Club the business men of lower Broadway tendered congratulations.

"Of course, it's a great surprise to us," Burdett and Sons would protest and wink heavily. "Of course, when the boy asked to be sent South we'd no idea he was planning to fight for Cuba! Or we wouldn't have let him go, would we?" Then again they would wink heavily. "I suppose you know," they would say, "that he's a direct descendant of General Hiram Greene, who won the battle of Trenton. What I say is, 'Blood will tell!'" And then in a body every one in the club would move against the bar and exclaim: "Here's to Cuba libre!"

When the Olivette from Key West reached Tampa Bay every Cuban in the Tampa cigar factories was at the dock. There were thousands of them and all of the Junta, in high hats, to read David an address of welcome.

And, when they saw him at the top of the gang-plank with his head in a bandage and his arm in a sling, like a mob of maniacs they howled and surged toward him. But before they could reach their hero the courteous Junta forced them back, and cleared a pathway for a young girl. She was travel-worn and pale, her shirt-waist was disgracefully wrinkled, her best hat was a wreck. No one on Broadway would have recognized her as Burdett and Sons' most immaculate and beautiful stenographer.

She dug the shapeless hat into David's shoulder.

She dug the shapeless hat into David's shoulder, and clung to him. "David!" she sobbed, "promise me you'll never, never do it again!"

THE BAR SINISTER

Preface

When this story first appeared, the writer received letters of two kinds, one asking a question and the other making a statement. The question was, whether there was any foundation of truth in the story; the statement challenged him to say that there was. The letters seemed to show that a large proportion of readers prefer their dose of fiction with a sweetening of fact. This is written to furnish that condiment, and to answer the question and the statement.

In the dog world, the original of the bull-terrier in the story is known as Edgewood Cold Steel and to his intimates as "Kid." His father was Lord Minto, a thoroughbred bull-terrier, well known in Canada, but the story of Kid's life is that his mother was a black-and-tan named Vic. She was a lady of doubtful pedigree. Among her offspring by Lord Minto, so I have been often informed by many Canadian dog-fanciers, breeders, and exhibitors, was the only white puppy, Kid, in a litter of black-and-tans. He made his first appearance in the show world in 1900 in Toronto, where, under the judging of Mr. Charles H. Mason, he was easily first. During that year, when he came to our kennels, and in the two years following, he carried off many blue ribbons and cups at nearly every first-class show in the country. The other dog, "Jimmy Jocks," who in the book was his friend and mentor, was in real life his friend and companion, Woodcote Jumbo, or "Jaggers," an aristocratic son of a long line of English champions. He has gone to that place where some day all good dogs must go.

In this autobiography I have tried to describe Kid as he really is, and this year, when he again strives for blue ribbons, I trust, should the gentle reader see him at any of the bench-shows, he will give him a friendly pat and make his acquaintance. He will find his advances met with a polite and gentle courtesy.

The Author.

PART I

The Master was walking most unsteady, his legs tripping each other. After the fifth or sixth round, my legs often go the same way.

But even when the Master's legs bend and twist a bit, you mustn't think he can't reach you. Indeed, that is the time he kicks most frequent. So I kept behind him in the shadow, or ran in the middle of the street. He stopped at many public houses with swinging doors, those doors that are cut so high from the sidewalk that you can look in under them, and see if the Master is inside. At night, when I peep beneath them, the man at the counter will see me first and say, "Here's the Kid, Jerry, come to take you home. Get a move on you"; and the Master will stumble out and follow me. It's lucky for us I'm so white, for, no matter how dark the night, he can always see me ahead, just out of reach of his boot. At night the Master certainly does see most amazing. Sometimes he sees two or four of me, and walks in a circle, so that I have to take him by the leg of his trousers and lead him into the right road. One night, when he was very nasty-tempered and I was coaxing him along, two men passed us, and one of them says, "Look at that brute!" and the other asks, "Which?" and they both laugh. The Master he cursed them good and proper.

But this night, whenever we stopped at a public house, the Master's pals left it and went on with us to the next. They spoke quite civil to me, and when the Master tried a flying kick, they gives him a shove. "Do you want us to lose our money?" says the pals.

I had had nothing to eat for a day and a night, and just before we set out the Master gives me a wash under the hydrant. Whenever I am locked up until all the slop-pans in our alley are empty, and made to take a bath, and the Master's pals speak civil and feel my ribs, I know something is going to happen. And that night, when every time they see a policeman under a lamp-post, they dodged across the street, and when at the last one of them picked me up and hid me under his jacket, I began to tremble; for I knew what it meant. It meant that I was to fight again for the Master.

I don't fight because I like fighting. I fight because if I didn't the other dog would find my throat, and the Master would lose his stakes, and I would be very sorry for him, and ashamed. Dogs can pass me and I can pass dogs, and I'd never pick a fight with none of them. When I see two dogs standing on their hind legs in the streets, clawing each other's ears, and snapping for each other's wind-pipes, or howling and swearing and rolling in the mud, I feel sorry they should act so, and pretend not to notice. If he'd let me, I'd like to pass the time of day with every dog I meet. But there's something about me that no nice dog can abide. When I trot up to nice dogs, nodding and grinning, to make friends, they always tell me to be off. "Go to the devil!" they bark at me. "Get out!" And when I walk away they shout "Mongrel!" and "Gutter-dog!" and sometimes, after my back is turned, they rush me. I could kill most of them with three shakes, breaking the backbone of the little ones and squeezing the throat of the big ones. But what's the good? They are nice dogs; that's why I try to make up to them: and, though it's not for them to say it, I am a street-dog, and if I try to push into the company of my betters, I suppose it's their right to teach me my place.

Of course they don't know I'm the best fighting bull-terrier of my weight in Montreal. That's why it wouldn't be fair for me to take notice of what they shout. They don't know that if I once locked my jaws on them I'd carry away whatever I touched. The night I fought Kelley's White Rat, I wouldn't loosen up until the Master made a noose in my leash and strangled me; and, as for that Ottawa dog, if the handlers hadn't thrown red pepper down my nose I never would have let go of him. I don't think the handlers treated me quite right that time, but maybe they didn't know the Ottawa dog was dead. I did.

I learned my fighting from my mother when I was very young. We slept in a lumber-yard on the river-front, and by day hunted for food along the wharves. When we got it, the other tramp-dogs would try to take it off us, and then it was wonderful to see mother fly at them and drive them away. All I know of fighting I learned from mother, watching her picking the ash-heaps for me when I was too little to fight for myself. No one ever was so good to me as mother. When it snowed and the ice was in the St. Lawrence, she used to hunt alone, and bring me back new bones, and she'd sit and laugh to see me trying to swallow 'em whole. I was just a puppy then; my teeth was falling out. When I was able to fight we kept the whole river-range to ourselves. I had the genuine long "punishing" jaw, so mother said, and there wasn't a man or a dog that dared worry us. Those were happy days, those were; and we lived well, share and share alike, and when we wanted a bit of fun, we chased the fat old wharf-rats! My, how they would squeal!

Then the trouble came. It was no trouble to me. I was too young to care then. But mother took it so to heart that she grew ailing, and wouldn't go abroad with me by day. It was the same old scandal that they're always bringing up against me. I was so young then that I didn't know. I couldn't see any difference between mother–and other mothers.

But one day a pack of curs we drove off snarled back some new names at her, and mother dropped her head and ran, just as though they had whipped us. After that she wouldn't go out with me except in the dark, and one day she went away and never came back, and, though I hunted for her in every court and alley and back street of Montreal, I never found her.

One night, a month after mother ran away, I asked Guardian, the old blind mastiff, whose Master is the night watchman on our slip, what it all meant. And he told me.

"Every dog in Montreal knows," he says, "except you; and every Master knows. So I think it's time you knew."

Then he tells me that my father, who had treated mother so bad, was a great and noble gentleman from London. "Your father had twenty-two registered ancestors, had your father," old Guardian says, "and in him was the best bull-terrier blood of England, the most ancientest, the most royal; the winning 'blue-ribbon' blood, that breeds champions. He had sleepy pink eyes and thin pink lips, and he was as white all over as his own white teeth, and under his white skin you could see his muscles, hard and smooth, like the links of a steel chain. When your father stood still, and tipped his nose in the air, it was just as though he was saying, 'Oh, yes, you common dogs and men, you may well stare. It must be a rare treat for you colonials to see real English royalty.' He certainly was pleased with hisself, was your father. He looked just as proud and haughty as one of them stone dogs in Victoria Park–them as is cut out of white marble. And you're like him," says the old mastiff–"by that, of course, meaning you're white, same as him. That's the only likeness. But, you see, the trouble is, Kid–well, you see, Kid, the trouble is–your mother—"

"That will do," I said, for then I understood without his telling me, and I got up and walked away, holding my head and tail high in the air.

But I was, oh, so miserable, and I wanted to see mother that very minute, and tell her that I didn't care.

Mother is what I am, a street-dog; there's no royal blood in mother's veins, nor is she like that father of mine, nor–and that's the worst–she's not even like me. For while I, when I'm washed for a fight, am as white as clean snow, she–and this is our trouble–she, my mother, is a black-and-tan.

When mother hid herself from me, I was twelve months old and able to take care of myself, and as, after mother left me, the wharves were never the same, I moved uptown and met the Master. Before he came, lots of other men-folks had tried to make up to me, and to whistle me home. But they either tried patting me or coaxing me with a piece of meat; so I didn't take to 'em. But one day the Master pulled me out of a street-fight by the hind legs, and kicked me good.

"You want to fight, do you?" says he. "I'll give you all the fighting you want!" he says, and he kicks me again. So I knew he was my Master, and I followed him home. Since that day I've pulled off many fights for him, and they've brought dogs from all over the province to have a go at me; but up to that night none, under thirty pounds, had ever downed me.

But that night, so soon as they carried me into the ring, I saw the dog was

overweight, and that I was no match for him. It was asking too much of a
puppy. The Master should have known I couldn't do it. Not that I mean to
blame the Master, for when sober, which he sometimes was–though not, as
you might say, his habit–he was most kind to me, and let me out to find food,
if I could get it, and only kicked me when I didn't pick him up at night and
lead him home.

But kicks will stiffen the muscles, and starving a dog so as to get him ugly-
tempered for a fight may make him nasty, but it's weakening to his insides,
and it causes the legs to wobble.

The ring was in a hall back of a public house. There was a red-hot
whitewashed stove in one corner, and the ring in the other. I lay in the
Master's lap, wrapped in my blanket, and, spite of the stove, shivering awful;
but I always shiver before a fight: I can't help gettin' excited. While the men-
folks were a-flashing their money and taking their last drink at the bar, a little
Irish groom in gaiters came up to me and give me the back of his hand to
smell, and scratched me behind the ears.

"You poor little pup," says he; "you haven't no show," he says. "That brute in
the tap-room he'll eat your heart out."

"That's what you think," says the Master, snarling. "I'll lay you a quid the Kid
chews him up."

The groom he shook his head, but kept looking at me so sorry-like that I begun
to get a bit sad myself. He seemed like he couldn't bear to leave off a-patting
of me, and he says, speaking low just like he would to a man-folk, "Well, good
luck to you, little pup," which I thought so civil of him that I reached up and
licked his hand. I don't do that to many men. And the Master he knew I didn't,
and took on dreadful.

"What 'ave you got on the back of your hand?" says he, jumping up.

"Soap!" says the groom, quick as a rat. "That's more than you've got on yours.
Do you want to smell of it?" and he sticks his fist under the Master's nose. But
the pals pushed in between 'em.

"He tried to poison the Kid!" shouts the Master.

"Oh, one fight at a time," says the referee. "Get into the ring, Jerry. We're
waiting." So we went into the ring.

I never could just remember what did happen in that ring. He give me no time
to spring. He fell on me like a horse. I couldn't keep my feet against him, and
though, as I saw, he could get his hold when he liked, he wanted to chew me

over a bit first. I was wondering if they'd be able to pry him off me, when, in the third round, he took his hold; and I begun to drown, just as I did when I fell into the river off the Red C slip. He closed deeper and deeper on my throat, and everything went black and red and bursting; and then, when I were sure I were dead, the handlers pulled him off, and the Master give me a kick that brought me to. But I couldn't move none, or even wink, both eyes being shut with lumps.

"He's a cur!" yells the Master, "a sneaking, cowardly cur! He lost the fight for me," says he, "because he's a — — — cowardly cur." And he kicks me again in the lower ribs, so that I go sliding across the sawdust. "There's gratitude fer yer," yells the Master. "I've fed that dog, and nussed that dog and housed him like a prince; and now he puts his tail between his legs and sells me out, he does. He's a coward! I've done with him, I am. I'd sell him for a pipeful of tobacco." He picked me up by the tail, and swung me for the men-folks to see. "Does any gentleman here want to buy a dog," he says, "to make into sausage-meat?" he says. "That's all he's good for."

Then I heard the little Irish groom say, "I'll give you ten bob for the dog."

And another voice says, "Ah, don't you do it; the dog's same as dead–mebbe he is dead."

"Ten shillings!" says the Master, and his voice sobers a bit; "make it two pounds and he's yours."

But the pals rushed in again.

"Don't you be a fool, Jerry," they say. "You'll be sorry for this when you're sober. The Kid's worth a fiver."

One of my eyes was not so swelled up as the other, and as I hung by my tail, I opened it, and saw one of the pals take the groom by the shoulder.

"You ought to give 'im five pounds for that dog, mate," he says; "that's no ordinary dog. That dog's got good blood in him, that dog has. Why, his father–that very dog's father—"

I thought he never would go on. He waited like he wanted to be sure the groom was listening.

"That very dog's father," says the pal, "is Regent Royal, son of Champion Regent Monarch, champion bull-terrier of England for four years."

"He's a coward, I've done with him."

I was sore, and torn, and chewed most awful, but what the pal said sounded so fine that I wanted to wag my tail, only couldn't, owing to my hanging from it.

But the Master calls out: "Yes, his father was Regent Royal; who's saying he wasn't? but the pup's a cowardly cur, that's what his pup is. And why? I'll tell you why: because his mother was a black-and-tan street-dog, that's why!"

I don't see how I got the strength, but, someway, I threw myself out of the Master's grip and fell at his feet, and turned over and fastened all my teeth in his ankle, just across the bone.

When I woke, after the pals had kicked me off him, I was in the smoking-car of a railroad-train, lying in the lap of the little groom, and he was rubbing my open wounds with a greasy yellow stuff, exquisite to the smell and most agreeable to lick off.

PART II

"Well, what's your name–Nolan? Well, Nolan, these references are satisfactory," said the young gentleman my new Master called "Mr. Wyndham, sir." "I'll take you on as second man. You can begin to-day."

My new Master shuffled his feet and put his finger to his forehead. "Thank you, sir," says he. Then he choked like he had swallowed a fish-bone. "I have a little dawg, sir," says he.

"You can't keep him," says "Mr. Wyndham, sir," very short.

"'E's only a puppy, sir," says my new Master; "'e wouldn't go outside the stables, sir."

"It's not that," says "Mr. Wyndham, sir." "I have a large kennel of very fine dogs; they're the best of their breed in America. I don't allow strange dogs on the premises."

The Master shakes his head, and motions me with his cap, and I crept out from behind the door. "I'm sorry, sir," says the Master. "Then I can't take the place. I can't get along without the dawg, sir."

"Mr. Wyndham, sir," looked at me that fierce that I guessed he was going to whip me, so I turned over on my back and begged with my legs and tail.

"Why, you beat him!" says "Mr. Wyndham, sir," very stern.

"No fear!" the Master says, getting very red. "The party I bought him off taught him that. He never learnt that from me!" He picked me up in his arms, and to show "Mr. Wyndham, sir," how well I loved the Master, I bit his chin and hands.

"Mr. Wyndham, sir," turned over the letters the Master had given him. "Well, these references certainly are very strong," he says. "I guess I'll let the dog stay. Only see you keep him away from the kennels–or you'll both go."

"Thank you, sir," says the Master, grinning like a cat when she's safe behind the area railing.

"He's not a bad bull-terrier," says "Mr. Wyndham, sir," feeling my head. "Not that I know much about the smooth-coated breeds. My dogs are St. Bernards." He stopped patting me and held up my nose. "What's the matter with his ears?" he says. "They're chewed to pieces. Is this a fighting dog?" he asks, quick and rough-like.

I could have laughed. If he hadn't been holding my nose, I certainly would have had a good grin at him. Me the best under thirty pounds in the Province of Quebec, and him asking if I was a fighting dog! I ran to the Master and hung down my head modest-like, waiting for him to tell my list of battles; but the Master he coughs in his cap most painful. "Fightin' dawg, sir!" he cries. "Lor' bless you, sir, the Kid don't know the word. 'E's just a puppy, sir, same as you see; a pet dog, so to speak. 'E's a regular old lady's lap-dog, the Kid is."

"Well, you keep him away from my St. Bernards," says "Mr. Wyndham, sir," "or they might make a mouthful of him."

"Yes, sir; that they might," says the Master. But when we gets outside he slaps his knee and laughs inside hisself, and winks at me most sociable.

The Master's new home was in the country, in a province they called Long Island. There was a high stone wall about his home with big iron gates to it, same as Godfrey's brewery; and there was a house with five red roofs; and the stables, where I lived, was cleaner than the aërated bakery-shop. And then there was the kennels; but they was like nothing else in this world that ever I see. For the first days I couldn't sleep of nights for fear some one would catch me lying in such a cleaned-up place, and would chase me out of it; and when I did fall to sleep I'd dream I was back in the old Master's attic, shivering under the rusty stove, which never had no coals in it, with the Master flat on his back on the cold floor, with his clothes on. And I'd wake up scared and whimpering, and find myself on the new Master's cot with his hand on the quilt beside me; and I'd see the glow of the big stove, and hear the high-quality horses below-stairs stamping in their straw-lined boxes, and I'd snoop the sweet smell of hay and harness-soap and go to sleep again.

The stables was my jail, so the Master said, but I don't ask no better home than that jail.

"Now, Kid," says he, sitting on the top of a bucket upside down, "you've got to understand this. When I whistle it means you're not to go out of this 'ere yard. These stables is your jail. If you leave 'em I'll have to leave 'em too, and over the seas, in the County Mayo, an old mother will 'ave to leave her bit of a cottage. For two pounds I must be sending her every month, or she'll have naught to eat, nor no thatch over 'er head. I can't lose my place, Kid, so see you don't lose it for me. You must keep away from the kennels," says he; "they're not for the likes of you. The kennels are for the quality. I wouldn't take a litter of them woolly dogs for one wag of your tail, Kid, but for all that they are your betters, same as the gentry up in the big house are my betters. I know my place and keep away from the gentry, and you keep away from the champions."

So I never goes out of the stables. All day I just lay in the sun on the stone flags, licking my jaws, and watching the grooms wash down the carriages, and the only care I had was to see they didn't get gay and turn the hose on me. There wasn't even a single rat to plague me. Such stables I never did see.

"Nolan," says the head groom, "some day that dog of yours will give you the slip. You can't keep a street-dog tied up all his life. It's against his natur'." The head groom is a nice old gentleman, but he doesn't know everything. Just as though I'd been a street-dog because I liked it! As if I'd rather poke for my vittles in ash-heaps than have 'em handed me in a wash-basin, and would sooner bite and fight than be polite and sociable. If I'd had mother there I couldn't have asked for nothing more. But I'd think of her snooping in the gutters, or freezing of nights under the bridges, or, what's worst of all, running through the hot streets with her tongue down, so wild and crazy for a drink that the people would shout "mad dog" at her and stone her. Water's so good that I don't blame the men-folks for locking it up inside their houses; but when the hot days come, I think they might remember that those are the dog-days, and leave a little water outside in a trough, like they do for the horses. Then we wouldn't go mad, and the policemen wouldn't shoot us. I had so much of everything I wanted that it made me think a lot of the days when I hadn't nothing, and if I could have given what I had to mother, as she used to share with me, I'd have been the happiest dog in the land. Not that I wasn't happy then, and most grateful to the Master, too, and if I'd only minded him, the trouble wouldn't have come again.

But one day the coachman says that the little lady they called Miss Dorothy had come back from school, and that same morning she runs over to the stables to pat her ponies, and she sees me.

"Oh, what a nice little, white little dog!" said she. "Whose little dog are you?" says she.

"That's my dog, miss," says the Master. "'Is name is Kid." And I ran up to her most polite, and licks her fingers, for I never see so pretty and kind a lady.

"You must come with me and call on my new puppies," says she, picking me up in her arms and starting off with me.

"Oh, but please, miss," cries Nolan, "Mr. Wyndham give orders that the Kid's not to go to the kennels."

"That'll be all right," says the little lady; "they're my kennels too. And the puppies will like to play with him."

You wouldn't believe me if I was to tell you of the style of them quality-dogs. If I hadn't seen it myself I wouldn't have believed it neither. The Viceroy of Canada don't live no better. There was forty of them, but each one had his own house and a yard–most exclusive–and a cot and a drinking-basin all to hisself. They had servants standing round waiting to feed 'em when they was hungry, and valets to wash 'em; and they had their hair combed and brushed like the grooms must when they go out on the box. Even the puppies had overcoats with their names on 'em in blue letters, and the name of each of those they called champions was painted up fine over his front door just like it was a public house or a veterinary's. They were the biggest St. Bernards I ever did see. I could have walked under them if they'd have let me. But they were very proud and haughty dogs, and looked only once at me, and then sniffed in the air. The little lady's own dog was an old gentleman bull-dog. He'd come along with us, and when he notices how taken aback I was with all I see, 'e turned quite kind and affable and showed me about.

"Jimmy Jocks," Miss Dorothy called him, but, owing to his weight, he walked most dignified and slow, waddling like a duck, as you might say, and looked much too proud and handsome for such a silly name.

"That's the runway, and that's the trophy-house," says he to me, "and that over there is the hospital, where you have to go if you get distemper, and the vet gives you beastly medicine."

"And which of these is your 'ouse, sir?" asks I, wishing to be respectful. But he looked that hurt and haughty. "I don't live in the kennels," says he, most contemptuous. "I am a house-dog. I sleep in Miss Dorothy's room. And at lunch I'm let in with the family, if the visitors don't mind. They 'most always do, but they're too polite to say so. Besides," says he, smiling most condescending, "visitors are always afraid of me. It's because I'm so ugly," says he. "I suppose," says he, screwing up his wrinkles and speaking very slow and impressive, "I suppose I'm the ugliest bull-dog in America"; and as he seemed to be so pleased to think hisself so, I said, "Yes, sir; you certainly are the ugliest ever I see," at which he nodded his head most approving.

"But I couldn't hurt 'em, as you say," he goes on, though I hadn't said nothing like that, being too polite. "I'm too old," he says; "I haven't any teeth. The last time one of those grizzly bears," said he, glaring at the big St. Bernards, "took a hold of me, he nearly was my death," says he. I thought his eyes would pop out of his head, he seemed so wrought up about it. "He rolled me around in the dirt, he did," says Jimmy Jocks, "an' I couldn't get up. It was low," says Jimmy Jocks, making a face like he had a bad taste in his mouth. "Low, that's what I call it–bad form, you understand, young man, not done in my set–and–and low." He growled 'way down in his stomach, and puffed hisself out, panting and blowing like he had been on a run.

"I'm not a street fighter," he says, scowling at a St. Bernard marked "Champion." "And when my rheumatism is not troubling me," he says, "I endeavor to be civil to all dogs, so long as they are gentlemen."

"Yes, sir," said I, for even to me he had been most affable.

At this we had come to a little house off by itself, and Jimmy Jocks invites me in. "This is their trophy-room," he says, "where they keep their prizes. Mine," he says, rather grand-like, "are on the sideboard." Not knowing what a sideboard might be, I said, "Indeed, sir, that must be very gratifying." But he only wrinkled up his chops as much as to say, "It is my right."

The trophy-room was as wonderful as any public house I ever see. On the walls was pictures of nothing but beautiful St. Bernard dogs, and rows and rows of blue and red and yellow ribbons; and when I asked Jimmy Jocks why they was so many more of blue than of the others, he laughs and says, "Because these kennels always win." And there was many shining cups on the shelves, which Jimmy Jocks told me were prizes won by the champions.

"Now, sir, might I ask you, sir," says I, "wot is a champion?"

At that he panted and breathed so hard I thought he would bust hisself. "My dear young friend!" says he, "wherever have you been educated? A champion is a–a champion," he says. "He must win nine blue ribbons in the 'open' class.

You follow me–that is–against all comers. Then he has the title before his name, and they put his photograph in the sporting papers. You know, of course, that I am a champion," says he. "I am Champion Woodstock Wizard III, and the two other Woodstock Wizards, my father and uncle, were both champions."

"But I thought your name was Jimmy Jocks," I said.

He laughs right out at that.

"That's my kennel name, not my registered name," he says. "Why, certainly you know that every dog has two names. Now, for instance, what's your registered name and number?" says he.

"I've got only one name," I says. "Just Kid."

Woodstock Wizard puffs at that and wrinkles up his forehead and pops out his eyes.

"Who are your people?" says he. "Where is your home?"

"At the stable, sir," I said. "My Master is the second groom."

At that Woodstock Wizard III looks at me for quite a bit without winking, and stares all around the room over my head.

"Oh, well," says he at last, "you're a very civil young dog," says he, "and I blame no one for what he can't help," which I thought most fair and liberal. "And I have known many bull-terriers that were champions," says he, "though as a rule they mostly run with fire-engines and to fighting. For me, I wouldn't care to run through the streets after a hose-cart, nor to fight," says he; "but each to his taste."

I could not help thinking that if Woodstock Wizard III tried to follow a fire-engine he would die of apoplexy, and seeing he'd lost his teeth, it was lucky he had no taste for fighting; but, after his being so condescending, I didn't say nothing.

"Anyway," says he, "every smooth-coated dog is better than any hairy old camel like those St. Bernards, and if ever you're hungry down at the stables, young man, come up to the house and I'll give you a bone. I can't eat them myself, but I bury them around the garden from force of habit and in case a friend should drop in. Ah, I see my mistress coming," he says, "and I bid you good day. I regret," he says, "that our different social position prevents our meeting frequent, for you're a worthy young dog with a proper respect for your betters, and in this country there's precious few of them have that." Then he waddles off, leaving me alone and very sad, for he was the first dog in many days that had spoke to me. But since he showed, seeing that I was a stable-dog, he didn't want my company, I waited for him to get well away. It was not a cheerful place to wait, the trophy-house. The pictures of the champions seemed to scowl at me, and ask what right such as I had even to admire them, and the blue and gold ribbons and the silver cups made me very miserable. I had never won no blue ribbons or silver cups, only stakes for the old Master to spend in the publics; and I hadn't won them for being a beautiful high-quality dog, but just for fighting—which, of course, as Woodstock Wizard III says, is low. So I started for the stables, with my head down and my tail between my legs, feeling sorry I had ever left the Master. But I had more reason to be sorry before I got back to him.

The trophy-house was quite a bit from the kennels, and as I left it I see Miss Dorothy and Woodstock Wizard III walking back toward them, and, also, that a big St. Bernard, his name was Champion Red Elfberg, had broke his chain and was running their way. When he reaches old Jimmy Jocks he lets out a roar like a grain-steamer in a fog, and he makes three leaps for him. Old Jimmy Jocks was about a fourth his size; but he plants his feet and curves his back, and his hair goes up around his neck like a collar. But he never had no show at no time, for the grizzly bear, as Jimmy Jocks had called him, lights on old Jimmy's back and tries to break it, and old Jimmy Jocks snaps his gums and claws the grass, panting and groaning awful. But he can't do nothing, and the grizzly bear just rolls him under him, biting and tearing cruel. The odds was all that Woodstock Wizard III was going to be killed; I had fought enough to see that: but not knowing the rules of the game among champions, I didn't like to interfere between two gentlemen who might be settling a private affair, and, as it were, take it as presuming of me. So I stood by, though I was shaking terrible, and holding myself in like I was on a leash. But at that Woodstock Wizard III, who was underneath, sees me through the dust, and calls very faint, "Help, you!" he says. "Take him in the hind leg," he says. "He's murdering me," he says. And then the little Miss Dorothy, who was crying, and calling to the kennel-men, catches at the Red Elfberg's hind legs to pull him off, and the brute, keeping his front pats well in Jimmy's stomach, turns his big head and snaps at her. So that was all I asked for, thank you. I went up under him. It was really nothing. He stood so high that I had only to take off about three feet from him and come in from the side, and my long "punishing jaw," as mother was always talking about, locked on his woolly throat, and my back teeth met. I couldn't shake him, but I shook myself, and every time I shook myself there was thirty pounds of weight tore at his wind-pipes. I couldn't see nothing for his long hair, but I heard Jimmy Jocks puffing and blowing on one side, and munching the brute's leg with his old gums. Jimmy was an old sport that day, was Jimmy, or Woodstock Wizard III, as I should say. When the Red Elfberg was out and down I had to run, or those kennel-men would have had my life. They chased me right into the stables; and from under the hay I watched the head groom take down a carriage-whip and order them to the right about. Luckily Master and the young grooms were out, or that day there'd have been fighting for everybody.

Well, it nearly did for me and the Master. "Mr. Wyndham, sir," comes raging to the stables. I'd half killed his best prize-winner, he says, and had oughter be shot, and he gives the Master his notice. But Miss Dorothy she follows him, and says it was his Red Elfberg what began the fight, and that I'd saved Jimmy's life, and that old Jimmy Jocks was worth more to her than all the St. Bernards in the Swiss mountains–wherever they may be. And that I was her champion, anyway. Then, she cried over me most beautiful, and over Jimmy Jocks, too, who was that tied up in bandages he couldn't even waddle. So when he heard that side of it, "Mr. Wyndham, sir," told us that if Nolan put me on a chain we could stay. So it came out all right for everybody but me. I was glad the Master kept his place, but I'd never worn a chain before, and it disheartened me. But that was the least of it. For the quality-dogs couldn't forgive my whipping their champion, and they came to the fence between the kennels and the stables, and laughed through the bars, barking most cruel words at me. I couldn't understand how they found it out, but they knew. After the fight Jimmy Jocks was most condescending to me, and he said the grooms had boasted to the kennel-men that I was a son of Regent Royal, and that when the kennel-men asked who was my mother they had had to tell them that too. Perhaps that was the way of it, but, however, the scandal got out, and every one of the quality-dogs knew that I was a street-dog and the son of a black-and-tan.

"These misalliances will occur," said Jimmy Jocks, in his old-fashioned way; "but no well-bred dog," says he, looking most scornful at the St. Bernards, who were howling behind the palings, "would refer to your misfortune before you, certainly not cast it in your face. I myself remember your father's father, when he made his début at the Crystal Palace. He took four blue ribbons and three specials."

But no sooner than Jimmy would leave me the St. Bernards would take to howling again, insulting mother and insulting me. And when I tore at my chain, they, seeing they were safe, would howl the more. It was never the same after that; the laughs and the jeers cut into my heart, and the chain bore heavy on my spirit. I was so sad that sometimes I wished I was back in the gutter again, where no one was better than me, and some nights I wished I was dead. If it hadn't been for the Master being so kind, and that it would have looked like I was blaming mother, I would have twisted my leash and hanged myself.

About a month after my fight, the word was passed through the kennels that the New York Show was coming, and such goings on as followed I never did see. If each of them had been matched to fight for a thousand pounds and the gate, they couldn't have trained more conscientious. But perhaps that's just my envy. The kennel-men rubbed 'em and scrubbed 'em, and trims their hair and curls and combs it, and some dogs they fatted and some they starved. No one talked of nothing but the Show, and the chances "our kennels" had against the other kennels, and if this one of our champions would win over that one, and whether them as hoped to be champions had better show in the "open" or the "limit" class, and whether this dog would beat his own dad, or whether his little puppy sister couldn't beat the two of 'em. Even the grooms had their money up, and day or night you heard nothing but praises of "our" dogs, until I, being so far out of it, couldn't have felt meaner if I had been running the streets with a can to my tail. I knew shows were not for such as me, and so all day I lay stretched at the end of my chain, pretending I was asleep, and only too glad that they had something so important to think of that they could leave me alone.

But one day, before the Show opened, Miss Dorothy came to the stables with "Mr. Wyndham, sir," and seeing me chained up and so miserable, she takes me in her arms.

"You poor little tyke!" says she. "It's cruel to tie him up so; he's eating his heart out, Nolan," she says. "I don't know nothing about bull-terriers," says she, "but I think Kid's got good points," says she, "and you ought to show him. Jimmy Jocks has three legs on the Rensselaer Cup now, and I'm going to show him this time, so that he can get the fourth; and, if you wish, I'll enter your dog too. How would you like that, Kid?" says she. "How would you like to see the most beautiful dogs in the world? Maybe you'd meet a pal or two," says she. "It would cheer you up, wouldn't it, Kid?" says she. But I was so upset I could only wag my tail most violent. "He says it would!" says she, though, being that excited, I hadn't said nothing.

So "Mr. Wyndham, sir," laughs, and takes out a piece of blue paper and sits down at the head groom's table.

"What's the name of the father of your dog, Nolan?" says he. And Nolan says: "The man I got him off told me he was a son of Champion Regent Royal, sir. But it don't seem likely, does it?" says Nolan.

"It does not!" says "Mr. Wyndham, sir," short-like.

"Aren't you sure, Nolan?" says Miss Dorothy.

"No, miss," says the Master.

"Sire unknown," says "Mr. Wyndham, sir," and writes it down.

"Date of birth?" asks "Mr. Wyndham, sir."

"I–I–unknown, sir," says Nolan. And "Mr. Wyndham, sir," writes it down.

"Breeder?" says "Mr. Wyndham, sir."

"Unknown," says Nolan, getting very red around the jaws, and I drops my head and tail. And "Mr. Wyndham, sir," writes that down.

"Mother's name?" says "Mr. Wyndham, sir."

"She was a–unknown," says the Master. And I licks his hand.

"Dam unknown," says "Mr. Wyndham, sir," and writes it down. Then he takes the paper and reads out loud: "'Sire unknown, dam unknown, breeder unknown, date of birth unknown.' You'd better call him the 'Great Unknown,'" says he. "Who's paying his entrance fee?"

"I am," says Miss Dorothy.

Two weeks after we all got on a train for New York, Jimmy Jocks and me following Nolan in the smoking-car, and twenty-two of the St. Bernards in boxes and crates and on chains and leashes. Such a barking and howling I never did hear; and when they sees me going, too, they laughs fit to kill.

"Wot is this–a circus?" says the railroad man.

But I had no heart in it. I hated to go. I knew I was no "show" dog, even though Miss Dorothy and the Master did their best to keep me from shaming them. For before we set out Miss Dorothy brings a man from town who scrubbed and rubbed me, and sandpapered my tail, which hurt most awful, and shaved my ears with the Master's razor, so you could 'most see clear through 'em, and sprinkles me over with pipe-clay, till I shines like a Tommy's cross-belts.

"Upon my word!" says Jimmy Jocks when he first sees me. "Wot a swell you are! You're the image of your grand-dad when he made his début at the Crystal Palace. He took four firsts and three specials." But I knew he was only trying to throw heart into me. They might scrub, and they might rub, and they might pipe-clay, but they couldn't pipe-clay the insides of me, and they was black-and-tan.

Then we came to a garden, which it was not, but the biggest hall in the world. Inside there was lines of benches a few miles long, and on them sat every dog in America. If all the dog snatchers in Montreal had worked night and day for a year, they couldn't have caught so many dogs. And they was all shouting and barking and howling so vicious that my heart stopped beating. For at first I thought they was all enraged at my presuming to intrude. But after I got in my place they kept at it just the same, barking at every dog as he come in: daring him to fight, and ordering him out, and asking him what breed of dog he thought he was, anyway. Jimmy Jocks was chained just behind me, and he said he never see so fine a show. "That's a hot class you're in, my lad," he says, looking over into my street, where there were thirty bull terriers. They was all as white as cream, and each so beautiful that if I could have broke my chain I would have run all the way home and hid myself under the horse trough.

All night long they talked and sang, and passed greetings with old pals, and the homesick puppies howled dismal. Them that couldn't sleep wouldn't let no others sleep, and all the electric lights burned in the roof, and in my eyes. I could hear Jimmy Jocks snoring peaceful, but I could only doze by jerks, and when I dozed I dreamed horrible. All the dogs in the hall seemed coming at me for daring to intrude, with their jaws red and open, and their eyes blazing like the lights in the roof. "You're a street dog! Get out, you street dog!" they yells. And as they drives me out, the pipe clay drops off me, and they laugh and shriek; and when I looks down I see that I have turned into a black-and-tan.

They was most awful dreams, and next morning, when Miss Dorothy comes and gives me water in a pan, I begs and begs her to take me home; but she can't understand. "How well Kid is!" she says. And when I jumps into the Master's arms and pulls to break my chain, he says, "If he knew all as he had against him, miss, he wouldn't be so gay." And from a book they reads out the names of the beautiful high-bred terriers which I have got to meet. And I can't make 'em understand that I only want to run away and hide myself where no one will see me.

Then suddenly men comes hurrying down our street and begins to brush the beautiful bull-terriers; and the Master rubs me with a towel so excited that his hands trembles awful, and Miss Dorothy tweaks my ears between her gloves, so that the blood runs to 'em, and they turn pink and stand up straight and sharp.

"Now, then, Nolan," says she, her voice shaking just like his fingers, "keep his head up–and never let the judge lose sight of him." When I hears that my legs breaks under me, for I knows all about judges. Twice the old Master goes up before the judge for fighting me with other dogs, and the judge promises him if he ever does it again he'll chain him up in jail. I knew he'd find me out. A judge can't be fooled by no pipe-clay. He can see right through you, and he reads your insides.

The judging-ring, which is where the judge holds out, was so like a fighting-pit that when I come in it, and find six other dogs there, I springs into position, so that when they lets us go I can defend myself. But the Master smooths down my hair and whispers, "Hold 'ard, Kid, hold 'ard. This ain't a fight," says he. "Look your prettiest," he whispers. "Please, Kid, look your prettiest"; and he pulls my leash so tight that I can't touch my pats to the sawdust, and my nose goes up in the air. There was millions of people a-watching us from the railings, and three of our kennel-men, too, making fun of the Master and me, and Miss Dorothy with her chin just reaching to the rail, and her eyes so big that I thought she was a-going to cry. It was awful to think that when the judge stood up and exposed me, all those people, and Miss Dorothy, would be there to see me driven from the Show.

The judge he was a fierce-looking man with specs on his nose, and a red beard. When I first come in he didn't see me, owing to my being too quick for him and dodging behind the Master. But when the Master drags me round and I pulls at the sawdust to keep back, the judge looks at us careless-like, and then stops and glares through his specs, and I knew it was all up with me.

"Are there any more?" asks the judge to the gentleman at the gate, but never taking his specs from me.

The man at the gate looks in his book. "Seven in the novice class," says he. "They're all here. You can go ahead," and he shuts the gate.

The judge he doesn't hesitate a moment. He just waves his hand toward the corner of the ring. "Take him away," he says to the Master, "over there, and keep him away"; and he turns and looks most solemn at the six beautiful bull-terriers. I don't know how I crawled to that corner. I wanted to scratch under the sawdust and dig myself a grave. The kennel-men they slapped the rail with their hands and laughed at the Master like they would fall over. They pointed at me in the corner, and their sides just shaked. But little Miss Dorothy she presses her lips tight against the rail, and I see tears rolling from her eyes. The Master he hangs his head like he had been whipped. I felt most sorry for him than all. He was so red, and he was letting on not to see the kennel-men, and blinking his eyes. If the judge had ordered me right out it wouldn't have disgraced us so, but it was keeping me there while he was judging the high-bred dogs that hurt so hard. With all those people staring, too. And his doing it so quick, without no doubt nor questions. You can't fool the judges. They see inside you.

But he couldn't make up his mind about them high-bred dogs. He scowls at 'em, and he glares at 'em, first with his head on the one side and then on the other. And he feels of 'em, and orders 'em to run about. And Nolan leans against the rails, with his head hung down, and pats me. And Miss Dorothy comes over beside him, but don't say nothing, only wipes her eye with her finger. A man on the other side of the rail he says to the Master, "The judge don't like your dog?"

"No," says the Master.

"Have you ever shown him before?" says the man.

"No," says the Master, "and I'll never show him again. He's my dog," says the Master, "and he suits me! And I don't care what no judges think." And when he says them kind words, I licks his hand most grateful.

The judge had two of the six dogs on a little platform in the middle of the ring, and he had chased the four other dogs into the corners, where they was licking their chops, and letting on they didn't care, same as Nolan was.

The two dogs on the platform was so beautiful that the judge hisself couldn't tell which was the best of 'em, even when he stoops down and holds their heads together. But at last he gives a sigh, and brushes the sawdust off his knees, and goes to the table in the ring, where there was a man keeping score, and heaps and heaps of blue and gold and red and yellow ribbons. And the judge picks up a bunch of 'em and walks to the two gentlemen who was holding the beautiful dogs, and he says to each, "What's his number?" and he hands each gentleman a ribbon. And then he turned sharp and comes straight at the Master.

"What's his number?" says the judge. And Master was so scared that he couldn't make no answer.

But Miss Dorothy claps her hands and cries out like she was laughing, "Three twenty-six," and the judge writes it down and shoves Master the blue ribbon.

I bit the Master, and I jumps and bit Miss Dorothy, and I waggled so hard that the Master couldn't hold me. When I get to the gate Miss Dorothy snatches me up and kisses me between the ears, right before millions of people, and they both hold me so tight that I didn't know which of them was carrying of me. But one thing I knew, for I listened hard, as it was the judge hisself as said it.

"Did you see that puppy I gave first to?" says the judge to the gentleman at the gate.

"I did. He was a bit out of his class," says the gate gentleman.

"He certainly was!" says the judge, and they both laughed.

But I didn't care. They couldn't hurt me then, not with Nolan holding the blue ribbon and Miss Dorothy hugging my ears, and the kennel-men sneaking away, each looking like he'd been caught with his nose under the lid of the slop-can.

We sat down together, and we all three just talked as fast as we could. They was so pleased that I couldn't help feeling proud myself, and I barked and leaped about so gay that all the bull-terriers in our street stretched on their chains and howled at me.

"Just look at him!" says one of those I had beat. "What's he giving hisself airs about?"

"Because he's got one blue ribbon!" says another of 'em. "Why, when I was a puppy I used to eat 'em, and if that judge could ever learn to know a toy from a mastiff, I'd have had this one."

But Jimmy Jocks he leaned over from his bench and says, "Well done, Kid. Didn't I tell you so?" What he 'ad told me was that I might get a "commended," but I didn't remind him.

"Didn't I tell you," says Jimmy Jocks, "that I saw your grandfather make his début at the Crystal—"

"Yes, sir, you did, sir," says I, for I have no love for the men of my family.

A gentleman with a showing-leash around his neck comes up just then and looks at me very critical. "Nice dog you've got, Miss Wyndham," says he; "would you care to sell him?"

"He's not my dog," says Miss Dorothy, holding me tight. "I wish he were."

"He's not for sale, sir," says the Master, and I was that glad.

"Oh, he's yours, is he?" says the gentleman, looking hard at Nolan. "Well, I'll give you a hundred dollars for him," says he, careless-like.

"Thank you, sir; he's not for sale," says Nolan, but his eyes get very big. The gentleman he walked away; but I watches him, and he talks to a man in a golf-cap, and by and by the man comes along our street, looking at all the dogs, and stops in front of me.

"This your dog?" says he to Nolan. "Pity he's so leggy," says he. "If he had a good tail, and a longer stop, and his ears were set higher, he'd be a good dog. As he is, I'll give you fifty dollars for him."

But before the Master could speak, Miss Dorothy laughs and says: "You're

Mr. Polk's kennel-man, I believe. Well, you tell Mr. Polk from me that the dog's not for sale now any more than he was five minutes ago, and that when he is, he'll have to bid against me for him."

The man looks foolish at that, but he turns to Nolan quick-like. "I'll give you three hundred for him," he says.

"Oh, indeed!" whispers Miss Dorothy, like she was talking to herself. "That's it, is it?" And she turns and looks at me just as though she had never seen me before. Nolan he was a-gaping, too, with his mouth open. But he holds me tight.

"He's not for sale," he growls, like he was frightened; and the man looks black and walks away.

"Why, Nolan!" cries Miss Dorothy, "Mr. Polk knows more about bull-terriers than any amateur in America. What can he mean? Why, Kid is no more than a puppy! Three hundred dollars for a puppy!"

"And he ain't no thoroughbred, neither!" cries the Master. "He's 'Unknown,' ain't he? Kid can't help it, of course, but his mother, miss–"

I dropped my head. I couldn't bear he should tell Miss Dorothy. I couldn't bear she should know I had stolen my blue ribbon.

But the Master never told, for at that a gentleman runs up, calling, "Three twenty-six, three twenty-six!" And Miss Dorothy says, "Here he is; what is it?"

"The Winners' class," says the gentleman. "Hurry, please; the judge is waiting for him."

Nolan tries to get me off the chain on to a showing-leash, but he shakes so, he only chokes me. "What is it, miss?" he says. "What is it?"

"The Winners' class," says Miss Dorothy. "The judge wants him with the winners of the other classes–to decide which is the best. It's only a form," says she. "He has the champions against him now."

"Yes," says the gentleman, as he hurries us to the ring. "I'm afraid it's only a form for your dog, but the judge wants all the winners, puppy class even."

We had got to the gate, and the gentleman there was writing down my number.

"Who won the open?" asks Miss Dorothy.

"Oh, who would?" laughs the gentleman. "The old champion, of course. He's won for three years now. There he is. Isn't he wonderful?" says he; and he points to a dog that's standing proud and haughty on the platform in the middle of the ring.

I never see so beautiful a dog–so fine and clean and noble, so white like he had rolled hisself in flour, holding his nose up and his eyes shut, same as though no one was worth looking at. Aside of him we other dogs, even though we had a blue ribbon apiece, seemed like lumps of mud. He was a royal gentleman, a king, he was. His master didn't have to hold his head with no leash. He held it hisself, standing as still as an iron dog on a lawn, like he knew all the people was looking at him. And so they was, and no one around the ring pointed at no other dog but him.

"Oh, what a picture!" cried Miss Dorothy. "He's like a marble figure by a great artist–one who loved dogs. Who is he?" says she, looking in her book. "I don't keep up with terriers."

"Oh, you know him," says the gentleman. "He is the champion of champions, Regent Royal."

The Master's face went red.

"And this is Regent Royal's son," cries he, and he pulls me quick into the ring, and plants me on the platform next my father.

I trembled so that I near fell. My legs twisted like a leash. But my father he never looked at me. He only smiled the same sleepy smile, and he still kept his eyes half shut, like as no one, no, not even his own son, was worth his lookin' at.

The judge he didn't let me stay beside my father, but, one by one, he placed the other dogs next to him and measured and felt and pulled at them. And each one he put down, but he never put my father down. And then he comes over and picks up me and sets me back on the platform, shoulder to shoulder with the Champion Regent Royal, and goes down on his knees, and looks into our eyes.

The gentleman with my father he laughs, and says to the judge, "Thinking of keeping us here all day, John?" But the judge he doesn't hear him, and goes behind us and runs his hand down my side, and holds back my ears, and takes my jaws between his fingers. The crowd around the ring is very deep now, and nobody says nothing. The gentleman at the score-table, he is leaning forward, with his elbows on his knees and his eyes very wide, and the gentleman at the gate is whispering quick to Miss Dorothy, who has turned white. I stood as stiff as stone. I didn't even breathe. But out of the corner of my eye I could see my father licking his pink chops, and yawning just a little, like he was bored.

The judge he had stopped looking fierce and was looking solemn. Something inside him seemed a-troubling him awful. The more he stares at us now, the more solemn he gets, and when he touches us he does it gentle, like he was patting us. For a long time he kneels in the sawdust, looking at my father and at me, and no one around the ring says nothing to nobody.

Then the judge takes a breath and touches me sudden. "It's his," he says. But he lays his hand just as quick on my father. "I'm sorry," says he.

The gentleman holding my father cries:

"Do you mean to tell me—"

And the judge he answers, "I mean the other is the better dog." He takes my father's head between his hands and looks down at him most sorrowful. "The king is dead," says he. "Long live the king! Good-by, Regent," he says.

The crowd around the railings clapped their hands, and some laughed scornful, and every one talks fast, and I start for the gate, so dizzy that I can't see my way. But my father pushes in front of me, walking very daintily, and smiling sleepy, same as he had just been waked, with his head high and his eyes shut, looking at nobody.

So that is how I "came by my inheritance," as Miss Dorothy calls it; and just for that, though I couldn't feel where I was any different, the crowd follows me to my bench, and pats me, and coos at me, like I was a baby in a baby-carriage. And the handlers have to hold 'em back so that the gentlemen from the papers can make pictures of me, and Nolan walks me up and down so proud, and the men shake their heads and says, "He certainly is the true type, he is!" And the pretty ladies ask Miss Dorothy, who sits beside me letting me lick her gloves to show the crowd what friends we is, "Aren't you afraid he'll bite you?" And Jimmy Jocks calls to me, "Didn't I tell you so? I always knew you were one of us. Blood will out, Kid; blood will out. I saw your grandfather," says he, "make his début at the Crystal Palace. But he was never the dog you are!"

For a long time he kneels in the sawdust.

After that, if I could have asked for it, there was nothing I couldn't get. You might have thought I was a snow-dog, and they was afeard I'd melt. If I wet my pats, Nolan gave me a hot bath and chained me to the stove; if I couldn't eat my food, being stuffed full by the cook—for I am a house-dog now, and let in to lunch, whether there is visitors or not,—Nolan would run to bring the vet.

It was all tommy rot, as Jimmy says, but meant most kind. I couldn't scratch myself comfortable, without Nolan giving me nasty drinks, and rubbing me outside till it burnt awful; and I wasn't let to eat bones for fear of spoiling my "beautiful" mouth, what mother used to call my "punishing jaw"; and my food was cooked special on a gas-stove; and Miss Dorothy gives me an overcoat, cut very stylish like the champions', to wear when we goes out carriage-driving.

After the next Show, where I takes three blue ribbons, four silver cups, two medals, and brings home forty-five dollars for Nolan, they gives me a "registered" name, same as Jimmy's. Miss Dorothy wanted to call me "Regent Heir Apparent"; but I was that glad when Nolan says, "No; Kid don't owe nothing to his father, only to you and hisself. So, if you please, miss, we'll call him Wyndham Kid." And so they did, and you can see it on my overcoat in blue letters, and painted top of my kennel. It was all too hard to understand. For days I just sat and wondered if I was really me, and how it all come about, and why everybody was so kind. But oh, it was so good they was, for if they hadn't been I'd never have got the thing I most wished after. But, because they was kind, and not liking to deny me nothing, they gave it me, and it was more to me than anything in the world.

It came about one day when we was out driving. We was in the cart they calls the dog-cart because it's the one Miss Dorothy keeps to take Jimmy and me for an airing. Nolan was up behind, and me, in my new overcoat, was sitting beside Miss Dorothy. I was admiring the view, and thinking how good it was to have a horse pull you about so that you needn't get yourself splashed and have to be washed, when I hears a dog calling loud for help, and I pricks up my ears and looks over the horse's head. And I sees something that makes me tremble down to my toes. In the road before us three big dogs was chasing a little old lady-dog. She had a string to her tail, where some boys had tied a can, and she was dirty with mud and ashes, and torn most awful.

She was too far done up to get away, and too old to help herself, but she was making a fight for her life, snapping her old gums savage, and dying game. All this I see in a wink, and then the three dogs pinned her down, and I can't stand it no longer, and clears the wheel and lands in the road on my head. It was my stylish overcoat done that, and I cursed it proper, but I gets my pats again quick, and makes a rush for the fighting. Behind me I hear Miss Dorothy cry: "They'll kill that old dog. Wait, take my whip. Beat them off her! The Kid can take care of himself"; and I hear Nolan fall into the road, and the horse come to a stop. The old lady-dog was down, and the three was eating her vicious; but as I come up, scattering the pebbles, she hears, and thinking it's one more of them, she lifts her head, and my heart breaks open like some one had sunk his teeth in it. For, under the ashes and the dirt and the blood, I can see who it is, and I know that my mother has come back to me.

I gives a yell that throws them three dogs off their legs.

"Mother!" I cries. "I'm the Kid," I cries. "I'm coming to you. Mother, I'm coming!"

And I shoots over her at the throat of the big dog, and the other two they sinks their teeth into that stylish overcoat and tears it off me, and that sets me free, and I lets them have it. I never had so fine a fight as that! What with mother being there to see, and not having been let to mix up in no fights since I become a prize-winner, it just naturally did me good, and it wasn't three shakes before I had 'em yelping. Quick as a wink, mother she jumps in to help me, and I just laughed to see her.

It was so like old times. And Nolan he made me laugh, too. He was like a hen on a bank, shaking the butt of his whip, but not daring to cut in for fear of hitting me.

"Stop it, Kid," he says, "stop it. Do you want to be all torn up?" says he. "Think of the Boston Show," says he. "Think of Chicago. Think of Danbury. Don't you never want to be a champion?" How was I to think of all them places when I had three dogs to cut up at the same time? But in a minute two of 'em begs for mercy, and mother and me lets 'em run away.

The big one he ain't able to run away. Then mother and me we dances and jumps, and barks and laughs, and bites each other and rolls each other in the road.

There never was two dogs so happy as we. And Nolan he whistles and calls and begs me to come to him; but I just laugh and play larks with mother.

"Now, you come with me," says I, "to my new home, and never try to run away again." And I shows her our house with the five red roofs, set on the top of the hill. But mother trembles awful, and says: "They'd never let me in such a place. Does the Viceroy live there, Kid?" says she. And I laugh at her. "No; I do," I says. "And if they won't let you live there, too, you and me will go back to the streets together, for we must never be parted no more." So we trots up the hill side by side, with Nolan trying to catch me, and Miss Dorothy laughing at him from the cart.

"The Kid's made friends with the poor old dog," says she. "Maybe he knew her long ago when he ran the streets himself. Put her in here beside me, and see if he doesn't follow."

So when I hears that I tells mother to go with Nolan and sit in the cart; but she says no–that she'd soil the pretty lady's frock; but I tells her to do as I say, and so Nolan lifts her, trembling still, into the cart, and I runs alongside, barking joyful.

When we drives into the stables I takes mother to my kennel, and tells her to go inside it and make herself at home. "Oh, but he won't let me!" says she.

"Who won't let you?" says I, keeping my eye on Nolan, and growling a bit nasty, just to show I was meaning to have my way.

"Why, Wyndham Kid," says she, looking up at the name on my kennel.

"But I'm Wyndham Kid!" says I.

"You!" cries mother. "You! Is my little Kid the great Wyndham Kid the dogs all talk about?" And at that, she being very old, and sick, and nervous, as mothers are, just drops down in the straw and weeps bitter.

Well, there ain't much more than that to tell. Miss Dorothy she settled it.

"If the Kid wants the poor old thing in the stables," says she, "let her stay."

"You see," says she, "she's a black-and-tan, and his mother was a black-and-tan, and maybe that's what makes Kid feel so friendly toward her," says she.

"Indeed, for me," says Nolan, "she can have the best there is. I'd never drive out no dog that asks for a crust nor a shelter," he says. "But what will Mr. Wyndham do?"

"He'll do what I say," says Miss Dorothy, "and if I say she's to stay, she will stay, and I say–she's to stay!"

And so mother and Nolan and me found a home. Mother was scared at first– not being used to kind people; but she was so gentle and loving that the grooms got fonder of her than of me, and tried to make me jealous by patting of her and giving her the pick of the vittles. But that was the wrong way to hurt my feelings.

That's all, I think. Mother is so happy here that I tell her we ought to call it the Happy Hunting Grounds, because no one hunts you, and there is nothing to hunt; it just all comes to you. And so we live in peace, mother sleeping all day in the sun, or behind the stove in the head groom's office, being fed twice a day regular by Nolan, and all the day by the other grooms most irregular. And as for me, I go hurrying around the country to the bench-shows, winning money and cups for Nolan, and taking the blue ribbons away from father.